Praise for *Roy of the Rovers*

"EPIC!"
– *Match of the Day Magazine*

"I love the way that they are about so much more
than football: they are about heart, values and family.
Both graphic novel and fiction titles are compelling,
engaging and a lot of fun. Lace up and get reading."
– Jim Sells, Programme manager for Sport & Literacy,
National Literacy Trust

"...has everything that today's children need as they
grow up. It is jam-packed with positive role models,
girls' involvement in Women's Football, respect, mental
well-being, good work ethic, education and aspiration."
– *Books for Topics*

"Packs a lot of punch in its short and simple to read
pages... It captures the feel of playing and having a
passion for football at an early age very well."
– *Comic Scene Magazine*

"I give it 5,000,000 stars. Amazing!"
– *The Book Brothers*

"I know already that it will be a popular title amongst
our football-loving children (not just boys!)."
– *That Boy Can Teach*

First published 2021 by Rebellion Publishing Ltd,
Riverside House, Osney Mead, Oxford, OX2 0ES, UK

ISBN: 978 1 78108 952 1

10 9 8 7 6 5 4 3 2 1

A CIP catalogue record for this book is available
from the British Library.

Printed in Denmark

Creative Director and CEO: Jason Kingsley
Chief Technical Officer: Chris Kingsley
Head of Publishing: Ben Smith
Publishing Manager: Beth Lewis
Editors: Bobby McGill & Olivia Hicks
Design: Sam Gretton
Cover image: Elkys Nova
Brand Manager: Bobby McGill

Follow us:

[Instagram] royoftheroversofficial [Facebook] royoftheroversofficial [Twitter] royoftherovers

www.royoftherovers.com   info@royoftherovers.com

In memory of Peter Nokes, 1933–1988

ROY REALISED THAT something unusual was going on even before he and Lofty had made it through the sliding doors of the Tayir Stadium's main entrance. There was a terrible racket coming from within the stadium.

But what was it?

As they walked into the lavish reception area of the Tayir, with its huge murals, glistening trophy cabinet and the smell of freshly ground coffee, it sounded like a bus load of football fans was somewhere inside the stadium corridors – where fans never went and were never supposed to go – and that they were chanting.

'What's going on?' Lofty asked, glancing at Roy.

The pair were close. They'd been friends since childhood and were now key players for the English Championship football outfit, Melchester Rovers. Living their childhood dream of playing football for the team they loved.

Roy shrugged, making out he wasn't bothered what the noise was. But he was bothered. Very bothered.

Because Roy Race liked things to be normal before a football match. He liked them to be the same, predictable, nothing off key. If anything *was* off key, he would begin to sense a creeping anxiety. The kind of anxiety that made it hard to concentrate on what you had to do.

Football.

Roy hated playing at Melchester Rovers' arch-rival's ground at the best of times. But here they were, at the Tayir Stadium, guests of Tynecaster United, while their own stadium – Mel Park – was being rebuilt after a fire.

And, what made it even worse, they had to be grateful for the honour of playing at the Tayir: Tynecaster United had offered them use of the stadium for free. It was a kind gesture that required the Melchester Rovers players to show respect and gratitude every time they set foot in there. Their enemies had been friends to them. How did you deal with that?

'Hi, Jatinder. Hi, Rebecca.'

Roy greeted the two staff on reception. That was how you dealt with it, he thought. Be friendly back. Be kind back. Make the world a nicer place.

Both receptionists waved at Roy, and made gestures that were difficult to interpret. Just then Roy noticed an extra security presence inside the stadium halls and corridors. Stewards everywhere. And still the roar of fans chanting.

Something was definitely up.

Roy and Lofty walked across the foyer of the reception area to the players' zone. Lofty opened the door so that he and Roy could access the changing rooms.

Now the noise hit them hard.

Chanting football fans. And inside. Definitely inside. Very close, too.

What was going on? Roy felt his unease growing. Things were not supposed to be like this.

Outside, moments before, Roy and Lofty had been enjoying a Tuesday evening in August. Warm air. Bright skies. Birds tweeting. Great preparation for the first cup tie of the season. Melchester Rovers had a home draw in the first round of the League Cup, the knockout competition open to teams in the Premier League, Championship, and Leagues One and Two.

The draw was good news for them. They

11

didn't have to go on a long bus journey or stay in a hotel, away from the familiarity of their own beds. And – in theory – they had the home advantage.

Except it wasn't really a home game because it wasn't at Mel Park.

But, even so, it shouldn't matter what stadium they were playing the game in. Melchester could not have had an easier draw. Crowley Harriers were just up from the Conference – after fifty years of non-league football – and in Division Two for the first time in their history. They were still semi-professional, with most of their players having other jobs. One was a postman. Another was an accountant. One was even a head teacher.

Rovers should win this one easily. Roy Race knew it and had known it all day. But all of the confidence Roy had been feeling was bleeding away now. The chaos. The mayhem.

Something was not right.

Lofty swore as the noise – and smell – of fifty or more football fans came wafting down the corridor. Loud and raucous. It reminded Roy of that gust of stale air that hits you when you're in the London Underground on a hot summer's day and a train rushes through the station. Sweaty and human.

He frowned. Roy needed routine. Not this. He needed to arrive at the stadium early. To sit in the changing rooms and listen to some music. To chat and smile with his teammates. To warm up in front of the gathering fans. Then a team talk from the Melchester Rovers boss, Kevin 'Mighty' Mouse.

Roy had enough on his plate with how things were at home. He didn't need other things to unsettle him.

Home. Home was hard. And it had been for three years.

Roy's dad was ill. He had a brain tumour. He could hardly speak anymore and was partially paralysed, along with other complications that meant Roy needed to be a carer for his dad, as well as a son. But Roy was happy with that. He could handle it. And he had been handling it for three years. It was just that things seemed to be getting worse recently.

Dad was becoming more confused. He wasn't able to move his body like he used to. He would stare into space. It was kind of like – sometimes – he wasn't there.

That was why Roy kept work and family separate. As long as things were steady at the club Roy could keep his tensions about his dad buried. It was like his job as a footballer was a bubble. Safe and airtight from the rest of his life.

Now that bubble was about to burst. Unless Roy worked out what was going on.

WALKING WITH A little less swagger, Roy and Lofty approached the home dressing room. The corridors of the Tayir Stadium were painted with images of Tynecaster's greatest footballers. Roy winked at the image of the Brazilian superstar, Hugo, who had become a friend in the last couple of years.

Then he noticed that a cluster of the Tayir Stadium security staff were standing outside the dressing room looking nervous.

'Evening, Bobby. Evening, Olivia,' Roy said cautiously.

He knew both stewards well. He made a

point of learning everybody's name and being polite. It was something his dad had always done at Mel Park and Roy was determined to be like his dad. Keep your feet on the ground and you won't lose your head in the clouds, Dad used to say, when he could speak. When he could walk. When he was well.

Roy brushed the thoughts about his dad away. He had to stop that. This evening was about football. 100% football.

'Lads,' Olivia said. 'There's... um... there's fifty Tynecaster fans occupying your dressing room and... we... well... how can I tell you this... we can't get them out.'

'Occupying?' Roy said.

'Like not coming out,' Bobby explained. 'Like refusing to come out until after the game in the hope of...'

'... making us lose,' Lofty finished Bobby's sentence.

'Yes,' Olivia smiled. 'That. I'm sorry, lads.'

Roy nodded and caught the eye of one of the Tynecaster fans, who pointed at Roy, then made an unpleasant gesture with his hand. Roy could feel his heart going too fast for pre-match. He really didn't want this.

'This club,' Lofty sighed.

'Yeah,' Roy replied.

This club. Tynecaster United. Whose owners had been wonderful. Whose fans had not. And Roy could see their point. Tynecaster fans hated it that Melchester played in their stadium. Wasn't that fair enough? He'd be appalled if Tynecaster played at their ground. The players dirtying the dressing rooms. The fans sitting in their seats. No one wanted that. But, then, no one had asked some maniac to burn down Mel Park last season.

'What now?' Lofty asked.

'We sort it,' Roy said, putting his hand on Lofty's shoulder.

'You sort it?' Olivia smiled. 'Really?'

'Yeah. Go on,' Roy grinned. 'Let me in.'

Olivia was chuckling now. 'You sure?'

Roy nodded. He could feel a touch of his anxiety from home – the stuff to do with Dad – coming through. He'd use that. His dad was coming to watch this game. And there was no way fifty unruly Tynecaster United fans were going to stop Roy playing football in front of his dad.

'Fine. Be my guest.' Olivia stood aside.

And, with that, Roy walked along a short corridor and into the occupied dressing room.

Twenty metres away from the Tynecaster fans.

Ten metres.

Five.

A plastic glass flew past Roy, beer spraying all over him.

But, not flinching, Roy kept going until he was face to face with the fans, who had stopped their chanting and raging.

Roy couldn't hear a thing now. The silence was crackling. But he could see every one of the Tynecaster fans was grinning. And that several had their mobile phones out, aimed at Roy.

Roy understood that, if this went wrong, he could be about to become the subject of a very embarrassing GIF that would be on every social media platform for a decade. But he didn't feel nervous. He felt determined. Determined that his dad would watch him play football.

'Please can we have the changing room?' he said to the large man in a blue and white striped Tynecaster top.

'Please can we have the changing room?' the man said back in a high-pitched voice.

An explosion of laughter hit Roy full in the face.

'I need to get my team in here,' Roy said. 'Kick off is in less than an hour.'

'I need to get my team in here,' the high-pitched voice echoed.

Then another voice. 'Kick off is in less than an hour.'

More laughter.

Roy knew he was going to get nowhere. He would not shift these fans. He felt a rush of anger. He took one step back, bumping into Lofty, who he now realised was right behind his shoulder. And now the Tynecaster fans began a new chant. Loud and fast. In Roy and Lofty's faces.

When I was just a little boy
I asked my mother what should I be.
Should I be Rovers?
Should I be Tyne?
Here's what she said to me...

Roy had had this for years. Tynecaster fans having a go at him being a Melchester supporter. What was it about them? They had no class. Half of them were glory supporters following a team that had been built by oil money. Tynecaster wasn't a proper football club. They had only ever known success and didn't understand humour and humility.

Like Roy's dad did.

Roy's dad had supported Melchester Rovers for decades. He had class. But this lot? Roy clenched his fists and took a step forward. Now he saw the look change in the eyes of the man in front of him. From smiling and goading to realising that Roy might be about to fight back.

And Roy welcomed it. He liked the feeling of wanting to make this man swallow his words.

The crowd of Tynecaster fans were quiet again. Roy could hear them breathing in, breathing out, breathing in, breathing out. But not backing down.

Roy was shocked at the situation he found himself in. With an hour to go before he had to captain his team in a major national cup competition that could take Melchester Rovers to a Wembley cup final, here he was, staring down a room of hostile Tynecaster fans. It was a stand-off. With neither him nor his opponents willing to back down.

But, still – in that moment – Roy was ready to take them all on. He didn't care about the

odds. He didn't care about being punched, kicked, injured. These fifty unsuspecting football fanatics had unbottled the fear and anger and confusion caused by his dad being ill. Fear and anger and confusion that he had been burying deep down inside himself week after week. Now all that turmoil was out in the open.

And it felt good.

To be angry.

Roy could smell the sweat of the three or four Tynecaster supporters he was face to face with now. They reeked like animals in a cage.

Feeling a sudden and uncontrollable surge of rage, Roy struck the door to his left with the palm of his hand.

'Come on then!' he shouted.

AFTER ROY'S OUTBURST of anger at the Tynecaster fans, there was another silence. A short one. That brief intake of breath before an explosion. Then Lofty was between Roy and the Tynecaster fans, his six-foot-four thick-set frame blocking the door.

Roy's friend was shaking his head.

'This isn't going to happen,' he said clearly, then swiftly took Roy by the shoulder, spun him round and dragged the captain of Melchester Rovers away from the fight.

And it was over. Roy let Lofty lead him away.

The Tynecaster United fans didn't follow.

There was no laughter. No goading. They were shocked that the golden boy of Melchester Rovers, Roy Race – who had never been sent off or even booked – had shown a wild side.

Roy felt weak. Like he had used up the day's energy – the week's energy – in a couple of minutes of madness.

What had come over him? Punching doors. He never did things like that. All this stuff to do with his dad: it was changing his personality. And the insane thing was that a part of him liked it. Even loved it. Usually *he* was the one calming people down, dealing with conflict.

All he could hear was his and Lofty's footsteps as they walked down the tight corridor away from their dressing room.

* * *

The Melchester Rovers team were directed to the groundsman's equipment room, directly beneath the main stand where fans would be gathering now.

Their new changing room.

Four walls, a ceiling, a floor made of cold grey concrete and twenty plastic bucket seats hastily collected for the players to sit on. Their manager, Kevin 'Mighty' Mouse, and first team coach, Johnny Dexter, were leaning against a giant sit-on lawnmower, muttering to each other.

Strange. It *was* strange to be getting ready for a match in a room full of lawnmowers. But not as strange as the rest of the scene playing itself out around Roy and Lofty.

Something else was wrong.

'Where's the rest of the team?' Roy snapped to Lofty. He still felt tense, like he could lose it at any moment.

Lofty studied the other players to see that he and Roy were, indeed, the only first team players in the makeshift changing rooms. The other twelve to fifteen bodies in there were the youth squad, all of them under eighteen, some as young as sixteen.

Lofty shrugged, like he didn't care. 'Listen, mate – you really need to calm down. You're not yourself. What's going on at home? Is it Rocky? Your dad? Or is it Ffion?'

Roy heard himself laugh manically. This was mad. And he really was not himself. The way he was laughing now. The way he'd faced down a room of fifty men. It was like he was outside himself and watching from across the room.

He put his hand on Lofty's shoulder. 'It's Dad,' he said gravely.

'Noted,' Lofty replied.

Now Johnny Dexter eased through the

room to be next to them.

'Lads.'

'Johnny,' Lofty and Roy said in unison.

'Change of plan,' their coach offered.

Roy glanced at the youth team players. They were stripped off. Some of them were putting on the red and yellow strips, socks. A couple were already tying their boots. Every now and then one of them would look over at Roy and Lofty in the same way fans looked at them on matchday or after training.

With awe.

Roy had worked out what was going on.

'Why are we fielding a team of kids?' he asked Coach so the other players couldn't hear.

Johnny Dexter's eyebrows furrowed.

'We're not. You two are playing,' he smiled helplessly.

Roy cast his eyes around the room.

'But no other first-teamers?' he asked.

Johnny shook his head. 'No. Just you two. Can I explain? And can we keep it between us, right?'

Lofty and Roy nodded.

'The chairperson…' Dexter paused. 'She… well… she's insisted we field a youth team in the League Cup. She says it'll give the young lads experience. Blood them. With you in defence, Peak. And you up front, Race.'

'But the truth is that she wants us out of the cup?' Lofty interrupted their coach.

'Now, I didn't say that,' Johnny said and frowned again.

'But it's the truth.'

Johnny smiled bitterly, but said nothing.

Now Roy understood everything. Penny Laine – their new chairperson, the daughter of the owner, only a year older than him, who had come in to run Melchester Rovers

– was picking the team above two of the most experienced men in football. Great. Just great.

But Roy didn't want to think about Penny Laine now. He could do that later. His thoughts went to the fans gathering in the stadium. His mum and dad and sister among them.

'They'll go mad,' Roy suggested.

'Who?'

'The fans, Johnny. They're paying full whack for this.'

Roy glanced at the youth players, who were watching the conversation. Listening too. Roy changed tack. He knew – as captain and senior player – he needed to appear calm and confident.

He could feel his head getting hot again.

Johnny Dexter nodded and spoke quietly. 'She's the boss.'

Roy closed his eyes.

'Right,' he muttered to himself. 'You're right.'

Now Roy turned to the youth team players. He knew them all. Everyone's names. He could see they were looking shaky, not sure if he was happy or unhappy. He had to turn this round. Kick off was in less than an hour.

'You all heard that, right?' Roy said.

Nods from the youth team.

And, as Roy studied them, he realised something. Even though he was nineteen and felt like a kid himself, he was not. These were the kids. Roy and Lofty were each about to record their one-hundredth appearance for Melchester Rovers and this lot hadn't played a first team game between them. They were about to face Crowley, a group of experienced fighters who had just emerged from non-league and would relish going toe-to-toe with a team with a history like Melchester Rovers.

'I'm not going to pretend I'm not confused,' Roy said.

He saw all eyes on him now. Even Mouse, stroking his chin, hoping Roy could turn this tricky situation round.

'So... some people might want us to slip out of the cup tonight so that we can concentrate on the league. But the fact is that doesn't have to happen. Does it?'

Roy was met with silence.

'So we go out there. We show our chairperson what we're made of. We win. Agreed?'

Several nods.

Roy was beginning to feel a little better. Like a leader again. That was what he needed to be today. More than ever.

'And I want you to know I am proud to be playing in a team with you. On the day most of you are making your debut for a team like Melchester Rovers. This is round one of the cup. Who wants to play in round two?'

Roy was shocked by the roar that came from the under-eighteens. It gave him hope. Maybe this team of youngsters – with him and Lofty on their side – could take this game by the scruff of the neck and win it.

ROY RAN ONTO the pitch ahead of the rest of his young teammates. After saluting the crowd, he looked around himself as the under-eighteen players warmed up, stroking the ball to and fro, stretching, some gazing into the crowd. Others were focused very much on the pitch.

Roy could see that the Melchester Rovers team looked slight compared to Crowley. It amazed him how young they appeared and it made him realise that the first team – himself and Lofty included – looked more like men than they had when they'd broken into the team in League Two just a couple of years ago.

And now, as they lined up to kick off, Roy smiled. Those were good memories. Maybe today would be okay. Maybe this was the next wave of young talent that was going to surprise the world of football like Melchester Rovers had two years before.

The referee blew his whistle as Melchester's two under-eighteen forwards kicked off, tapping the ball between them, then looking up to play a pass.

The next sound was a thud as a Crowley player scythed into the young Melchester striker, taking his legs and leaving him curled up in pain on the half-way line, howling with pain.

The crowd roared in protest and the referee blew his whistle again, to pull out a yellow card. The ball hadn't even left the centre circle.

The player who'd committed the foul was still smiling. He winked at Roy.

'Job done,' he remarked.

So that was it. Roy understood. Crowley were going to play hard and rough with the hope of scaring Roy's teammates to death – or at least defeat.

Roy called to the other players. 'Come on. Let's do this. They think they can scare us, but that's not going to happen. Agreed?'

Roy didn't get much of a reaction to his call to arms. And, as the Rovers' youth striker was stretchered off, the remaining young players looked even more like boys. And Roy could see they were afraid.

Roy could see quite easily that most of the young Rovers players were scared of the tackle. And why shouldn't they be? Man for man, the opposition were so much bigger than them. It really was men against boys. Every time Roy tried to push Melchester forward, one of his teammates lost the ball, shying away from an inevitable crunching tackle they'd all seen demonstrated so well in the first seconds of the match.

The game would not play out well if this carried on. Roy knew that. It didn't take long for brutality to pay off for Crowley, and for his fears to be realised.

Crowley won possession easily on the edge of their own penalty area after a Melchester attack petered out. As the Rovers midfield stood off, the Crowley centre back hoofed a long ball up the pitch. It travelled sixty or seventy yards and was followed up by the first-minute fouler, who shouldered his way through two half tackles and smacked the ball home.

0–1.

An easy goal. Almost unchallenged. It was ugly football. But it worked.

The second Crowley goal was more subtle.

Another long ball from the back, the League Two team packed the box with players, with one trailing his leg out as a Melchester tackle came in.

He went down screaming. A clear case of diving. All the Crowley player's teammates stopped and pointed at the penalty spot, demanding a spot kick.

The ref's whistle – which was beginning to fill Roy with dread – sounded again.

Penalty.

Roy was desperately trying to think ahead to what Crowley's next move would be. Suddenly, as Roy watched the Crowley captain sidle up to Melchester's willowy keeper, he knew. They were going to try and put the keeper off his game. Roy rushed over and stood in between his keeper and the captain, then stared at the ref.

'Are you going to give my players any protection at all, ref?' Roy demanded.

'You're the ones giving away a penalty,' the ref said.

Roy shook his head. He thought of something to say to the ref. It included the word *cheating*. But he didn't. He knew better than to push referees too far. He might end up with a yellow card and that would make the game even harder to claw back.

One step back, then the penalty taker

drove the ball into the net.

0–2.

Roy felt sick. As he gathered the ball, trying to gee up his teammates with positive words, he glanced over at his dad by the front of the pitch, where wheelchair-users sat in a specially heated area.

Dad was staring at his hands.

Roy wasn't quite sure how to interpret that. Was his dad defeated by the fact Rovers were losing 2–0 at home to a team fifty places below them in the footballing world? Or was he feeling ill? Then Roy noticed his mum wave him away, telling him to focus on the game. Mum was right, of course. What was Roy doing? He never lost his focus like this. He thought back to the incident in the dressing room and wondered how much that face-to-face with the Tynecaster fans had taken from him. He felt like he had no control over anything today.

The game went on. Long balls, hard tackles, referee-baiting from the opposition. Roy and Lofty did their best to rouse their players, but, not knowing who needed a kick or who needed an arm round the shoulder, it was hard to get through to them.

Roy remained calm and kind throughout. But when the third goal went in – a header resulting from a corner – he wondered if he was getting it all wrong. Perhaps he should be shouting at them.

3–0 down with half time approaching, Roy began to doubt whether the last chance of a comeback had already gone.

THE YOUNG MELCHESTER Rovers side walked off the pitch, heads hung low after a first half that had been a mismatch. A bunch of sixteen- and seventeen-year-olds against a tough, well-drilled team of hard men who'd fought their way out of non-league and into the big time.

Melchester 0 Crowley 3.

Down the tunnel went the players. Out of the glare of the floodlights that felt more like spotlights on a stage, or searchlights in a prison camp. Into the corridors – past photographs of Tynecaster United players holding trophies and medals that Roy and his new teammates could only dream of.

The home fans hadn't booed. They applauded gently. Trying to be kind to the team of mostly debutants. Trying not to show how disappointed they were that Melchester had fielded a below-strength team and were probably about to be giant-killed.

Avoiding looking at his family as he passed them, Roy had done his best to encourage the youngsters as they came off the Tayir Stadium pitch. He heard himself say things like *Keep doing what you're doing* and *This is all about experience. Let's learn from our disappointments.* But he found it hard to take himself seriously.

The young players responded well.

'Thanks, Roy.'

'I will. I'll do better in the second half, Roy.'

Roy caught Mouse's eye as they nearly collided in the tunnel, heading back into the home dressing room, which had now been cleared of Tynecaster fans, even though it still smelled of them.

Mouse studied Roy as the team slumped onto their benches, heads down as Johnny passed round energy drinks. Roy took a long drink and tried to feel energetic, but it was difficult. All that nonsense before the match with the Tynecaster fans had thrown him off his game. He'd let himself down, let Melchester Rovers down. Plus the frustration that the chairperson had been happy to throw this game. Roy felt again like he'd used up his week's energy and he had nothing left to give.

Now Mouse was standing over him.

'Roy?'

'Boss?'

Mouse had raised his voice, so the whole team could listen in.

'Tell us what it was like two years ago when you were thrown in at the deep end against Kingsbay. Your debut.'

All eyes on Roy now.

And Roy knew what Mouse was up to. He wanted Roy to be a role model, to inspire them, to make them believe that they could live Roy's dream.

Roy was happy to play along.

'We got battered,' Roy smiled. 'We were young, inexperienced. Like you lot. Playing against hard men trying to scare the hell out of us. But it was still the proudest day of my life. My debut. My first time in this shirt. You never forget that.'

Roy could see the tired faces of his young teammates turn to him. He knew he had a chance to affect them now, to give them heart. They might not win this game, but they needed to face the second half – and come away from it – with pride. As he spoke, he could feel his own pride and determination returning.

'We were kids,' Roy recalled. 'The same age as you. We had no first team appearances between us. And we got bullied and laughed at. People used that old line "You'll win nothing with kids", but we kept at it. We stood together and we wore this badge with pride.'

Roy pulled his Melchester Rovers badge tight.

'Look. The chances are for one or two of you this might be your only ever professional game. And the chances are that one or two of you might just be first-teamers in the Championship by the end of the season. But you have to decide – regardless of the fact we're three–nil down – which you want to be. I took my chance and it paid off. What do you want?'

'Good,' Mouse said, looking to Lofty now. 'Lofty? What about you?'

Lofty smiled and looked at Roy. 'Like what he said. You don't know where that first step is going to lead to, but you give it your all. You could end up at Real Wherever and lift the World Cup for your country.

Or you could end up back at college, your contract cancelled. It's a lottery, football. But you're the only one who can buy a ticket for you. And that starts here.'

The young squad were all sat on the edge of their seats now. Leaning forward, eyes eager.

Roy could see the effect his and Lofty's words had had on his young teammates. They were fired up. It was in their eyes. Maybe – he thought – they could turn a three-goal deficit over?

THE SECOND HALF against Crowley started better. Mouse had shuffled the team, dropping Roy back into midfield to take control, putting a young striker called Noel Baxter, who had just come off the bench, up front.

'Play the ball into space ahead of Noel,' Johnny said to Roy. 'Measure your passes right and he'll be onto it. You'll be pleasantly surprised.'

It didn't take Roy long to spot what Johnny had been getting at.

Speed.

Boy, was Noel Baxter fast.

Over five or six yards he seemed to have the supernatural ability to lose his man with outrageous acceleration. And that one talent, combined with a good touch, is dynamite.

The game felt different now. With Roy in midfield and Lofty bossing the defence, Melchester seemed to have a grip on the game. They'd put a young winger – called Rahim Dollar – out wide, too. A great outlet to release pressure.

On fifty-two minutes, Lofty intercepted a long Crowley ball and played it to Roy's feet. Roy took it, turned, beat the first man, looked up to see Noel Baxter this side of the Crowley defensive line, coiled like a spring.

Worth a go, Roy thought to himself, slotting a diagonal ball in between the two opposition defenders with a flick of his left foot, then powering forward into the Crowley half.

Noel Baxter was onto the ball before the two defenders had put their arms up appealing for offside, even though it wasn't.

The flag stayed down and now it was a race. Baxter in on goal. Roy to his left, staying onside to receive the pass. The keeper coming out, hesitating on the six-yard line.

But then the net was bulging. And Roy didn't understand. He'd been expecting a pass, to slot it home. But somehow – without Roy even seeing him pull the trigger – Noel Baxter had hammered the ball past the Crowley keeper.

Now there was some crowd noise. Excitement. Encouragement.

1–3 down. The fans sensed a comeback.

Roy jogged over to Noel and shook his

hand. He remembered – years ago – how his captain from Grimroyd on the moor had shaken his hand when he'd scored his first senior goal. It had made him feel good, part of the team. So he did the same.

'Keep doing that,' Roy said.

'I will,' Noel Baxter beamed.

Kick off again and Crowley had changed their shape. Roy was surprised to see they were playing with a libero, also known as a sweeper, a defender who can go where he wants, but tends to play behind the defence. This, to counteract Baxter's pace.

At first Roy was fascinated. He'd never played against a sweeper before. It was quite an old-fashioned tactic. But – as the player who was trying to pick the locks of the Crowley defence – it soon went from being fascinating to frustrating. Every ball Roy put through was cut out by the sweeper.

And – pacey though he was – Noel Baxter could not get on the end of Roy's passes.

Eighty-one minutes on the clock and Roy found himself on the break, coming over the half-way line, the Crowley defence backing off.

Roy had options. The through-ball to Noel Baxter. Or to play it to one of the wingers on either side of him – Rahim Dollar on the right and a lad called Jeremy playing too far out on the left to be able to have an impact on the game. But, so far, both had squandered any passes he'd played into them.

Thirty yards out, with the sweeper poised to cut his next pass out, Roy saw the keeper was a touch too far off his line and he hit it without thinking.

Instinctive.

Left-footed.

Hard.

The ball slammed onto the underside of the bar, bounced on the goal line and spun back into play, where Noel Baxter, waiting, leaped into the air and headed the ball down hard, off the six-yard line and into the net.

Goal. Outstanding goal. And now – after a hesitation of surprise in the stands – there was noise. A roar that echoed around the stadium.

'Come on, Rovers... Come on, Rovers... Come on, Rovers...' echoed from the stands.

Melchester had clawed the game back from 0–3 to 2–3. One more goal and there'd be extra time and penalties. This was winnable.

'Come on,' Roy shouted. 'We can do this.'

The deep-defending long-ball brutal-battering tactics of Crowley were suddenly not working. The League Two team looked more non-league. Their tackling calamitous.

Three minutes into injury time and Roy fired a pass into Noel Baxter, who ran towards goal, ready to release a shot. One touch. Two touches. Then Noel was down, scythed by an appalling tackle. So bad the defender didn't even wait for the referee to show a red card, walking off like a batsman who knows he's been caught.

As Roy lined up the free kick, a second Crowley player was sent off for pushing the ref.

But Roy remained calm. He stood alongside Noel Baxter as the rows went on between ref, linesman and the opposition.

'Ignore it,' Roy coached. 'Keep calm. Just stare at the goal. At the keeper too. Let him know that you're not ruffled.'

Noel did as Roy suggested.

Eventually the referee restored order. The Crowley wall lined up for the free kick. Twenty yards out.

'Fancy it?' Roy asked Noel, the pair of them standing over the ball.

Noel shook his head. He looked pale suddenly. And Roy understood the pressure that must put a player under. The last kick of the game. If you don't score, your team is out of the cup to a lower league opposition.

On your debut.

Roy eyed the keeper again. 'It's okay,' he said. 'I've got this. But next time it's your turn, yeah?'

'Yeah,' Noel Baxter replied.

Roy heard the ref's whistle. Eyed the keeper one more time. Took five steps back, then ran at the ball, hit it, curled it round the wall, over the keeper's leap, to see it smack the crossbar and ricochet into the away fans behind the goal.

He'd missed.

The whistle blew. It was over.

Melchester Rovers were out of the cup.

The final score: Melchester Rovers 2 Crowley 3.

Roy was gutted and angry. But he still went round each of the young players who'd worn red and yellow to praise them on their second-half performance, as the Crowley players ran to their fans and celebrated the giant-killing.

Roy went over to congratulate as many of the Crowley players as he could. The last one was the Crowley libero. Close up he looked about twenty-nine, nearly a decade older than Roy.

'Well played,' Roy said.

'Thanks,' the player replied. 'You too. Listen, mate. Please can I have your shirt?'

'Sure,' Roy replied, surprised. 'So long as I can have yours. Listen… I thought you played the sweeper so well tonight. You pulled our tactics up at the roots. Well done.'

Another handshake and then Roy went over to see his family. Lofty joined him, always keen to speak to Roy's mum and dad and Rocky. But what Roy saw immediately started to make him feel uneasy. Mum was bent over Dad's wheelchair, fussing. Rocky staring at Roy.

'Dad's gone a bit... quiet,' his sister told him, hand on his chest, stopping him from interrupting Mum and Dad.

'What do you mean?' Roy whispered, wishing he'd paid his family more attention during the game.

'He's just not... you know, like before.'

Roy knew what his sister was saying. When Dad had first become ill – a brain tumour, stopping him from being able to work the kettle or turn a tap, lots of small things – he had sometimes gone quiet, stared into space. That was what Rocky meant. Mum stood up. 'Let's all get home, shall we?'

It wasn't a question.

'I'll get your kit bag,' Lofty said. 'Give me two minutes, I'll bring it to your car.'

61

Then he was off, leaving Roy and Rocky to help Mum get Dad to the car, parked inside the perimeter of the stadium.

None of them spoke. They didn't need to. This was confirmation of their worst fears. Dad's health – after two years of his illness being under control and manageable – was deteriorating.

THE LAST THREE years had been tough for Roy. Although they had seen him go from Sunday morning park footballer to Championship striker, making his wildest dreams come true and more, they had also been the hardest of his life.

His dad had been ill.

Very ill.

At first Dad had struggled to remember words or how to put a spoon in a coffee jar. It seemed really trivial, but the doctor had sent him for a scan. Just in case something was wrong.

And there was.

Very wrong. Dad had a brain tumour: a cancer growing inside his skull, squashing and squeezing his brain, messing with his ability to move and speak and even think.

Next he had had an operation to try to remove it. But the operation went wrong. Dad was partially paralysed and barely able to speak. He would never be able to do those things again. Life had changed for him and his family.

A series of unfortunate events.

But they'd lived with it. Mum, Dad, Roy and Rocky.

They'd had a chairlift fitted at home.

They'd got used to Dad in a wheelchair, barely saying a word. It had become normal and they were still happy as a family.

Why not? They were together. They were safe. They had love. They had football. And football had been at the centre of Roy and Dad's life before he was ill, and remained so now. Watching Melchester Rovers at Mel Park or on TV. Playing FIFA in the front room. Reading newspapers and magazines together. And – now that Roy played for the team they both loved – Dad would come to the ground to watch him in action.

Life could be good.

But it could be bad too. And it had been getting worse recently.

Dad wasn't able to come to as many games now. He had days when he could barely lift himself from his wheelchair to the sofa. He went a week without saying a word.

Not good.

At home Roy found it hard. He loved his dad. He loved his mum. He loved his sister, Rocky, too. But now he was finding that football – rather than being the thing that brought him and his dad together – was Roy's escape from the weight of the world on his shoulders, the darkening mood at home.

He needed – sometimes – to escape.

He felt guilty about it sometimes, but he always felt happier when he was leaving the house to go to work. To get away from the pressure and the worry and just kick a ball around.

With Mum and Rocky, Roy got Dad home and into bed. Then he had a cup of tea with Mum in the kitchen.

'I don't like how things are going, Roy,' Mum said.

Roy shook his head.

'What shall we do?' he asked.

'I think… I think, if anything else like this happens, we need to speak to the hospital again.'

Roy nodded. 'I think so too,' he said.

THE NEXT DAY there was a full training session for the first team squad. Roy and Lofty were offered the chance of a recovery day after playing a full ninety minutes the night before. A day off where they could sit and watch the deadline day transfer deals being done on the TV, feet up. One of the most interesting days in the football calendar, where desperate teams signed desperate players in a frenzy of media-fuelled madness.

He declined the chance of a day watching the TV. There was a match to be played on Saturday. An away game against Medway

Rangers in the Championship.

There was no time for recovery now they had to concentrate on the league. And Roy wanted to work hard. The harder he pushed himself at work, the less time he spent thinking about home.

Regardless of the defeat the night before, first team spirit was positive. And with good reason: after seven games in the Championship, Melchester Rovers were mid-table, doing great for a newly promoted side. But they all knew that one defeat might pitch them towards danger. They could not rest. Not really relax.

Roy had clocked that Vic Guthrie – his co-captain – had worn a smile on his face all morning. Why was that? he wondered. He would have to wait to find out. But Roy had a good idea what was afoot. Vic loved to wind people up. Especially Roy.

'Okay. Spit it out. What?' Roy asked, having tripped Vic on purpose, as he broke away with the ball.

Vic grinned. 'What do you mean *what*?'

Roy narrowed his eyes. He could sense other players were listening as they took a break. Frankie Pepper, the team's physio, was among them passing out drinks.

'What's so funny?'

'Oh...' Vic was speaking in his loud listen-to-me voice. 'I just wanted to know something. That's all, mate.'

'What?' Roy sighed.

'What it feels like,' Vic said.

Roy felt a shudder of anger. But he knew to keep it to himself. With wind up like this you had to play it calm, give nothing away, find something funny to say so that you come out on top. But he knew this was going to be about last night, the cup defeat. So, he decided to pre-empt Vic.

'What *what* feels like, Vic?' Roy smiled back. 'Not to be dropped? To have played all the first team games this season? Unlike yourself. Is that what's puzzling you? Mate?'

Vic smiled and nodded as the first team clustered round to listen. Vic versus Roy was always fun.

'To be giant-killed,' Vic said. 'To lose to a non-league team. What must that feel like? Shameful? Humiliating? Share with us, Roy. Please.'

As Vic was rambling on, Roy caught sight of a blue Porsche 911 drawing up in the car park on the other side of the training ground fence. He could have sworn it was Will Gray's car. His school mate and former striking partner, now an England international at top flight Islington. But he put it out of his mind.

'Roy?' Vic goaded. 'I asked what it feels like.'

'Devastating,' Roy replied and covered his face. Then he went down on his haunches. 'I can't...' he moaned. 'I can't cope... I just.' He pretended to cry.

When Roy felt Vic's hand on his shoulder, he knew he had him.

'Sorry, mate,' Vic coughed. 'I didn't... I'm sorry... I...'

Roy sprang back to his feet, facing Vic, a big grin on his face.

Vic folded his arms. The rest of the team were laughing at him now, not at Roy.

Job done.

Vic 0 Roy 1.

THEY SPENT THE rest of the morning on set pieces.

'We all know that anyone can beat anyone in this league,' Johnny Dexter said. 'Teams are evenly matched. The difference between those that will win this weekend and those that will lose: what is it?'

'Desire?' Zhang Wei called out.

'Fitness?' Patrick Nolan added.

'No, you idiots,' Johnny Dexter said.

'Desire? Fitness? My God, I hope you all have that at one hundred per cent all the time. No, I'm talking about set pieces. Corners. Free kicks. Penalties. That's where it's at. This is what we're doing. I want attack versus defence. Ten different set piece scenarios. Ten times each. Then that team meeting you're all looking forward to.'

'Where's Mouse?' Gordon Stewart, the team's goalie, asked.

'Buying a new keeper for deadline day,' Vic snapped.

'Busy,' Johnny Dexter replied, staring darkly at Vic.

'Busy doing what?' Gordon pushed.

'Selling you if you don't stop asking bloomin' questions,' Johnny replied. 'Now, leave the grown-up stuff to the grown-ups and get on with some work.'

Roy liked set piece training. It was like

playing in a highlights reel. Just the main attacks, none of the ball being passed around between the penalty areas. It was *all* penalty area action.

Volleys.

Headers.

Chesting the ball down, laying it off to another teammate.

Testing the central defenders, Lofty and Vernon.

And the bonus was that if one of the defenders was doing well, making it impossible for Roy to score, it was a positive. It meant Melchester Rovers had a good defence.

In total they took a hundred free kicks and corners.

By the end Roy was shattered. The muscles in his neck feeling it from headers and his thighs stiff. That was his fault. A full training session less than twenty-four hours after a game. He suspected Mouse wouldn't have let that happen, but Dexter was old school. Roy wasn't even sure he'd know what recovery meant.

At the end of training Johnny Dexter again reminded the team of the meeting. Roy wondered what it could be about. If a team meeting was in the changing rooms, it was normal: tactics, football, on the pitch stuff. If it was in a hospitality suite, it meant more. It meant that the club's owners were involved. Off the pitch stuff.

As THEY WALKED over to the changing rooms for the team meeting, Vic came and put his arm round Roy.

'You miss her, don't you? Ffion.'

Roy was on guard, was this another wind

up? Vic was relentless today, so Roy decided to play it straight. As always.

'I do,' he said.

'Me too.'

They walked a few paces in silence.

'You don't seem yourself, mate,' Vic tried again. 'I wondered if it was because you're missing my sis.'

Roy nodded. So he didn't seem himself. That was no surprise, considering what was going on at home. But Roy was determined to keep it buried at work. He wanted work to be free of all those things, a place he could be himself.

'Must be,' Roy said. 'But I'll live. Things change every day: you just have to accept it and push on.'

'Change,' Vic mused. 'You're right. There's no getting away from it.'

Roy and Vic walked side by side towards

the changing rooms, stretching their legs as they did. Lunging. On tiptoes. Easing out the efforts of the last two hours.

From high up in the offices – rebuilt after the fire – a solitary figure watched the first team coming off the training pitches. The chairperson. Penny Laine. She was standing with two young male figures, both in tracksuits, one of them pointing down at Roy and Vic.

'This team meeting?' Roy asked, back down on the turf.

'What about it?' Vic said.

'Any ideas?'

Vic shook his head, then opened his mouth to speak.

'What?' Roy knew Vic had a theory.

'Transfer deadline day' Vic speculated.

Roy chewed his lip. 'Could be that.'

'Let's hope so,' Vic joked. 'Think we need

a new striker after that shambles last night. Losing to a non-league team? Embarrassing. I am so glad I wasn't part of that.'

THEY GATHERED IN the new conference centre that had been built during the closed season. A huge white marquee with central heating and an area for press interviews. And – although it was a temporary structure – once you were inside, it felt like a normal building. More like an office block than a giant plastic tent.

As the players made their way in, Roy noticed the rest of the club's staff were there. The office workers. Those who manned reception. The grounds staff. The ticket office staff. Even some of the matchday managers.

'This is big,' Lofty said, nudging Roy. 'Whatever *this* is.'

Roy nodded. His friend was right. They'd never been spoken to altogether as a football club. The players alongside everyone else. And he decided that he liked it. Everyone together like this. Whatever you did at the club you were part of the team, the success, as far as Roy was concerned. Roy nodded to and shook the hands of several of the club's staff as he and Lofty found a seat next to Nadiya and Phil who worked in the club kitchens.

Now Roy noticed that Penny Laine was standing at the front, greeting people from a metal and glass lectern as the club employees gathered, chatting to them, shaking hands with the few who approached her on the stage. At the back of the stage area was a set of panels. Roy thought he saw shadows moving behind them.

Penny reminded Roy of a vicar at a church service. The calm demeanour. The respect from those who came to greet her. There was a massive sense of expectation now and Roy thought he saw Penny catch his eye, smile, then look away. But he was probably imagining it.

Roy was distracted from his thoughts about Penny by a tap on his shoulder. Asif Mirza was behind him. And Dan Pacanowski.

'What is this?' Asif asked.

Roy shrugged. 'No idea.'

The last people to come into the hall were Johnny Dexter and Kevin Mouse, who sat in one of the reserved seats on the front row.

Silence fell.

Penny smiled, took a breath, then began. 'We are gathered here today…'

Most of the audience laughed. The tension

was broken in five words. Roy immediately had respect for Penny's speaking skills.

'... because we have some very important announcements to make,' she went on. 'Announcements that will affect the future of Melchester Rovers, its fans and its employees – you – very much.'

Roy sensed the tension returning. He heard someone say she'd not seen anything on the club website about this. Changes? What changes?

Penny put her hands up. 'Please... don't worry. These changes... they will affect you – all of us – but in a good way. And we wanted you to know first. Before the media. Before the fans. Let me explain.'

Penny took another deep breath.

'We are planning to run Melchester Rovers in a new way, based on the model of ownership popular at Atletico Cervantes and Borussia Goethe. We are going to hand ownership of the club to the fans.'

Roy sat forward. 'What?' he said to himself.

'Decisions made by the club,' Penny explained, 'and investments in the future will be directed by the fans. Club bonds – owned by the fans – will be handed down from mothers to sons, fathers to daughters. Together, we will invest in the infrastructure of the club, the academy, and on that note, I am thrilled to announce today that we have agreed a deal to adopt Sowerby FC, turn them into Melchester Women's Football Club, and welcome them into the Mel Park family.'

Now there was chatter in the room as Penny paused to speak to someone behind the panel that was shielding whoever was standing there – hidden – on stage with her.

Just who was behind the screen? That was what everyone was asking.

Roy took the opportunity to text Rocky.

Am at club meeting. You're going to be a Mel Rovers player.

A reply came back immediately.

Wot?

Penny was talking again now. Roy listened as he filled Rocky in on the news by text.

'We want to build a team for the future,' Penny Laine said. 'It is not a coincidence that we are modelling ourselves on two of the great and historic giants of the European game. Melchester Rovers have been part of that history and – with your help – we will be again. Together.'

Penny paused.

'And we must be sure that we are all together on this. No one player can ever be bigger than the club. This is about the club and its fans. The club and its city.'

Roy finished his text and looked up to see Penny eyeing him again, aware that other staff were looking at him too. He felt like he had been caught on his phone by a teacher at school. That sharp shock of shame.

Penny lowered her voice. 'We will have no Billy Big Boots at Melchester Rovers,' she said, then grinned as Roy was slapped on the back of his head by Asif and Dan, and Lofty rolled back in his seat, laughing.

Roy felt himself blush. He slipped his phone into his pocket.

Penny leaned into the microphone, enjoying Roy's discomfort.

'Is Rocky pleased with the news?' she asked.

Roy nodded and tried to smile.

'Good,' Penny said. 'You can tell her we intend to build a team around her in the future.'

More laughter.

'I mean it,' Penny said. 'Tell her.'

Roy – aware all eyes were on him – retrieved his phone and texted Rocky the message. He had the weirdest feeling. Pride. He was proud of his sister: that she was in Penny's plans to create a Melchester Rovers women's team.

Says she wants to build a team around you.

A reply came back from Roy's sister. Roy laughed.

'What did she say?' Penny asked.

'Nothing.'

'No... share the joke with us.'

Roy stared at the single word Rocky had pinged back at him. He wasn't going to say that in front of everyone. He thought for a moment how best to answer. Thought – too – about this woman who seemed always to be on his case, winding him up, smiling and catching his eye. He really had no idea how to deal with Penny Laine.

The things she had just told them were amazing and something he could never dream of for his club: to be a European giant again, to be run well, not like Tynecaster and all those other football clubs run by international billionaires.

But then she made him feel cross too. Putting him on the spot like this.

Penny Laine. She did his head in. Did he like her? Did he dislike her? He couldn't make his mind up.

'Well?' Penny was insisting on an answer.

Roy decided to give Penny some of her own medicine.

'She says…' Roy repeated Rocky's word.

The rest of the audience fell about with laughter.

And now Roy could see that Penny was flushed red. She stood embarrassed for a few seconds, then cleared her voice, smiling again.

'Touché,' she said to Roy. 'But now it's my turn to put you on the back foot, Roy Race. Well… all of you, in fact.'

Another mumble of anticipation. And – with the heat off him – Roy studied the room. He could tell the staff of Melchester Rovers liked their new owner. Penny Laine was open, generous and had a sense of humour.

Roy liked her, he decided. He was amazed how someone not more than a year older than him could be so at ease speaking in front of an audience.

'Most football clubs do their transfer dealings in the full glare of the media. No player is ever signed without speculation in the media. But we want to be different. We believe that bringing in new players needs to be done in a calm manner, without other clubs trying to muscle in. Which is why – right now – we would like to introduce you to two new players and a new manager.'

The gasp that went up from Penny Laine's audience surprised even her.

Then questions in the audience. Dozens of them.

'Who?'

'Players?'

'A new manager... what?'

THERE WAS AN intake of breath when three figures walked out to join Penny on the raised platform. Then silence. For a moment.

Until Roy broke it.

'Blackie,' he gasped and jumped from his seat to embrace his friend, quickly followed by his teammates. Roy couldn't stop himself: his best mate was home and wearing Mel Rovers' red and yellow. His strike partner from two seasons ago when the dream began.

'Call me Will, mate. I think I've grown past that nickname.'

A stocky young man with highlighted hair and an older woman stood with Penny on the stage watching the scrum of young men welcoming Will Gray back to Mel Park.

'Roy, sit,' Penny spoke into the microphone. 'You're spoiling the theatre of it.'

Roy released his best friend. The players returned to their seats and calm returned. Will Gray was grinning ear to ear after his welcome.

'Now… where were we?' Penny said, smiling, but irritated, Roy could see. 'It is *my* great pleasure to welcome our three new signings…'

Roy studied the trio as Penny introduced them.

He could hardly sit still, looking at Will Gray. Mates since children. It was only a year since Will had signed for top flight Islington. And now – Penny had explained – he was back on a season-long loan.

Next up was Serina Heracles, the manager of the Dutch women's football team. Until now. Now she was here to manage Melchester Women, Penny told them. Or Sowerby FC. Roy couldn't believe it. Here was one of Europe's greatest football coaches coming to Melchester.

He texted his sister.

Serina Heracles.

Legend. What about her?

She's your new boss.

Not waiting for a reply – and enjoying how much that would wind up his sister – Roy put his phone away for the final introduction. The third figure on the stage.

But Roy didn't need an introduction. He recognised the player. Roy had had him on his FIFA team for a season. A midfield dynamo. And he'd seen him as much on the front pages of the tabloids as the back over the last year or two.

'Now please let me introduce... Wonderkid. Megastar of the future. Jimmy Slade.'

Another round of applause. Not quite

as enthusiastic as the one for Heracles, Roy noted. Roy understood why there was a mixed reaction to Slade. The man came with a reputation.

Jimmy Slade flicked his hair away from his eyes and saluted his new teammates.

Roy felt someone move in close behind him. Vic.

'What's he doing here? He was with Inter Tremezzo, the disgraced Italian football giants, wasn't he? The ones who bribed refs for fifty years and won everything?'

'He was,' Roy replied quietly. 'But he's not anymore. He's here.'

'Bit of a handful, I heard,' Vic added. 'I was told that he has some weird habits. Like, he shows up at training in fancy dress and he once climbed on top of one of the stands the night before a match, then shouted all sorts of abuse at his teammates for the whole game. And there was nothing anyone could do.'

Lofty butted in. 'I heard he went into a rival club's shop and bought a load of scarves and shirts and took them out into the town square, doused them in petrol and burned them.'

Roy shook his head. He had heard all these stories, but never knew whether to believe them. If Slade was so wild, why had Mouse signed him?

'Why *have* we signed him then?' Roy gave his thoughts voice.

'He's a genius. Like a modern-day Maradona,' Vic explained.

'And you know the new owner is an agent too? Penny Laine?' Lofty added. 'She's his agent. Know what I mean?'

Roy understood what he was feeling. It was transfer deadline day. Across the country groups of footballers would be meeting new teammates and worrying whether those new players would take their place in the team at the same time as thinking it was a good thing that their club was bringing in new players.

Things changed. Roy knew that. Better players would come in. All he had to focus on was being the best that he could be. And leave the rest to fate.

Will drove Roy the short distance home in his Porsche 911. Roy leaned back in the seat and wondered if he should learn to drive. It'd be nice to have a car. He could drive his dad to and from his appointments instead of Mum. That'd help her.

'Why didn't you tell me you were coming back?' Roy asked.

Will shifted up a gear, as they moved onto the ring road.

'I was sworn to secrecy. That Penny. She said "Tell no one. Especially Race. I know you're mates."'

Roy shook his head. 'She's a cool customer,' he mused.

'Yeah,' Will said. 'Then she started asking me about you. It was weird. I think she's got a file on you. She badgered me about Ffion. Wanted to know if you two were still an item.'

'So where are you staying?' Roy asked, changing the subject. He didn't want to talk about Ffion. 'Not your mum's?'

'No. She's away anyway. I am at the hotel at the Tayir.'

'Oof,' Roy said. 'How horrible.'

Will smiled.

'Come home for tea?' Roy suggested.

Will burst out laughing. 'Like when we were kids? Playing football all day, then your mum doing fish fingers, chips and beans?'

'Yeah. Exactly. Come on.'

*　　*　　*

WHEN THEY WERE inside, all sat round the table in the kitchen, Roy did feel like a kid again.

Rocky and Will squabbling.

Dad laughing.

Mum smiling.

Sometimes Roy wished life was all like that again. Being ten. Playing football for fun. Eating fish fingers.

But not anymore.

Now the club had a dietician who gave Roy a list of what he could eat and when. Tonight it was steamed fish and rice for everyone, not fish fingers and chips. With three veg: green (beans, not baked), red (beetroot) and orange. Roy wasn't sure what the orange was. He just ate it. Like he did in the club canteen.

Roy was relieved he was earning more money now Melchester Rovers were in the Championship, so that – as well as paying for his dad's care and with his mum not working at all now – he could pay for all the fresh fish and veg. It cost a lot more than a box of fish fingers and a tin of beans. He'd also paid for a new roof on the house, double glazing throughout and a car for Mum that would make it easier for her to get Dad in and out.

'So are you going to get a place to live, William?' Mum was asking Will questions.

'I dunno,' Will said. 'The hotel's nice and it

makes life easy. I mean… if it becomes more than a loan… maybe…'

As Will spoke, everyone was aware that Dad was struggling with a fish finger. (He was allowed fish fingers.) It was like he was trying to catch it with his fork, but he kept missing. As if the fish finger was moving. But no one mentioned it as Mum subtly helped Dad to get the fork to his mouth.

'So have you heard anything about Heracles?' Will asked Rocky. 'Have the club talked to you yet?'

Chewing, mouth full, Rocky shook her head.

'I heard that she wants top flight football the year after next,' Will went on. 'She's obsessed with making the women's team the best in Europe, before the men are, even.'

Rocky grinned at Roy. 'I might be in the top flight before you, Roy,' she teased.

'Not if I can help it,' Roy replied.

Brother and sister glanced at Dad. Dad liked a bit of banter between Roy and Rocky. It entertained him. But today his head was down. Almost like he was asleep.

Realising what was going on, Mum stood up.

'Right. You pair go through. Rocky, help me with your dad.' Then she raised her voice. 'Might be a good time to get you to bed, Danny?'

AN HOUR LATER, Dad in bed, Roy stood on the doorstep with Mum, waving Will off. Will beeped the horn, then his Porsche purred as it moved carefully down the long terraced street.

'Good to have him back?' Mum asked, her arm round Roy's shoulder.

Roy nodded. 'How's Dad?'

Mum didn't reply.

'Mum?'

A cold breeze ruffled the trees outside the front door and Roy shut it, to keep the warmth in.

'Not great,' Mum answered at last. 'But you know that. He seems a bit... anyway... I'm going to call his consultant. He said to call day or night if I had any questions. So I'll just see what he thinks.'

'Good idea,' Roy said, feeling a deep ache in his guts. He knew it wasn't the fish he'd just eaten: it was dread.

IT STARTED ON the bikes in the warm-up room pre-training. They had a new gym now, under one of the new stands. A large space with bicycle machines and other equipment all laid out in a heated room. The plan was for them to get their muscles working by moving and stretching inside before they hit the cold air outside. It led to fewer injuries.

Roy liked it. It gave him focus. Although today most of the squad's focus had been taken by Jimmy Slade.

It was difficult not to stare as the new boy went faster and faster on his bike, legs pumping, wearing a cowboy hat and waving it in the air like he was in some old American Western film. He had arrived at the club for training – inexplicably – dressed as a cowboy and was now making whooping noises as if he was rounding up a herd of cattle.

'Where did he get a cowboy kit?' Roy asked Lofty, as they warmed up on the gym mats together.

Lofty shrugged. 'No idea,' he said. 'And why bring it all in to work?'

Patrick Nolan and Vernon Elliott were with Slade, laughing along. Bonding. Roy knew it was important for new players to become part of the banter, to gel with the others. He was just surprised at how Jimmy Slade went about it.

He smiled. Well, half smiled. Jimmy Slade was a player he wasn't sure about yet. He was one of those who made a lot of noise.

The kind that wanted to be the centre of attention. And sometimes that was good. Every team needed its loudmouths, its chaos causers, its comedians. It helped everyone deal with the pressure.

But sometimes these things backfired.

The warm-up room was great, built with easy access to the edge of the training areas. Another new space erected in recent days by the new owners of Melchester Rovers, who had insisted on making sure the players had state-of-the-art training facilities and could warm up inside even before they started running on the fields. Floor-to-wall windows out onto the fields. Water stations. Massage tables. It was the works. It was top flight. And Roy loved it.

At the back of the indoor area, a row of eight warm-up bikes gleamed, silver and black. Six running machines ran in parallel. Then an area of mats – red and yellow – on the floor where Roy, Will and Lofty were stretching and now watching as Nat Gosden, the old man of the team, approached the cowboy, Jimmy Slade.

'Take it easy, Jimmy,' Nat advised. 'Don't

burn all your energy up. Save it for when we're on the training fields. They work us hard here.'

Jimmy Slade slowed the pace of his cycling, then stopped. He put his cowboy hat on, then, with his finger, lifted its brim and studied the older player.

Roy could sense trouble even before Slade replied.

'I'm the new boy in town,' Slade said in an American drawl, rubbing his cheek. 'You got a problem with new boys?'

Nat Gosden glanced around him. The noises of bikes and running machines had whirred to a halt. Everyone was waiting for Nat's response.

Roy liked Gosden. He'd played in the top flight for a decade, represented England in two World Cups. The kind of player that you automatically respected. And – after a few teething problems on his arrival – he was a great guy to have around. Part of the Melchester Rovers set up.

But Jimmy Slade hadn't got that memo.

The fifteen footballers waited for Gosden's response. One that needed to be good. The older footballer had to put the upstart in his place.

Nat Gosden narrowed his eyes. 'Well, I'm the Sheriff. The *old* boy. The kind who puts up with a lot until, one day, he snaps.'

Gosden stared at Slade until the younger man looked away, smiling, and the noise of machines whirring started up again.

Game over. For now. But Roy knew they'd not seen the last of that clash. He looked over at Vic Guthrie, jogging slowly on a running machine. Vic and Roy were co-captains. Each nodded to the other to acknowledge they'd seen and were aware of the new rivalry forming between Gosden and Slade.

Now Mouse and Dexter appeared in the doorway.

'Come on, lads. On the fields. Pronto.'

Training.

EIGHTY MINUTES LATER and into the last phase of training.

Set pieces again.

Free kicks. Attackers against defenders. This, after over an hour of breathless running, tackling, passing and close-quarter action, gave the players a chance to chat as they waited for their turn to hammer the ball at Gordon Stewart's goal, protected by a wall of Lofty, Elliot, MacKay, Vic and Mirza.

Roy had noticed – all morning – that Will was not going into tackles like he used to.

Roy and Will had played football since they could walk. And one of Will's signatures was that he would want to win any and every ball, whatever it took. And that part of his game had vanished.

Roy decided to raise it with Will.

'Do you want to talk about it?' Roy asked.

'About what, mate?'

'Tackling.'

Will's face clouded over briefly, then he smiled.

'Not really,' he said.

Roy nodded. 'Well, I'm here when you do.'

Will smiled. 'I know. I hear you. It's just… it'll take time.'

'Is it the injury you got last season?'

'Maybe… I dunno. I go for the ball and it's like my legs just…' Will made a groaning noise and Roy saw his best friend's career ahead of him. A striker who would go for every challenge. Playing in the top flight. Picked for England.

Fearless. Fearsome. Natural.

And then it was lost.

It all came back to Roy. His own injury the season before last. How he'd lost that careless way of playing. The way you play when you've never been hurt, never been on the sidelines for weeks fearing your career is over.

'Can I tell you something?' Roy asked, after both he and Will had hammered the ball over the wall at Gordon's goal one last time, walking back to the changing rooms now.

'Go on.'

'I think it's like a mental block that you can't think your way out of.'

'Eh?'

Roy frowned. It was hard to put into words. 'Look… when I was injured and struggled to come back, I knew I had to get stuck in, but I couldn't get my head to tell my legs what to do… so I kind of let my legs do the thinking. I'm not being much help… what I mean is… you have to stop thinking about stuff and just do it.'

Will shook his head. 'I get that,' he said. 'In theory. It's just doing it on the pitch. But thanks. Thanks for trying to help.'

'Do it in training. Just throw yourself around. It'll come.'

'I will. Cheers, mate. Anyway, listen, how's your dad? Was he okay last night?'

'Your dad?' Lofty asked, joining them now. 'He okay?'

Roy shrugged and his mind went to Mum calling his dad's consultant that morning. He wondered if she'd got through. What had been said? Damn. He didn't want to think about this. Not here.

'Fine,' he said, blanking his friends' questions. 'I need a warm down.' Roy started a slow jog back to the changing rooms.

Not Dad. Not here. Going round and round his head. But his mind was on his mobile phone in his locker. Was there a message from Mum on there?

To say she'd spoken to the consultant.

Roy forced himself to think about Will's tackle-shyness instead. And how he could help him. His mind tracked back through training. Will's shooting and passing was better than ever. He was so sharp. Stronger, too. But when it came to the tackle he'd lost it. Maybe no one else had spotted it, as none of the team knew Will as well as Roy did, but it was there and it explained why Will Gray was back at Melchester Rovers.

He'd dropped a division. His top flight parent club wanted him to get his old self back in the Championship. That was obvious. And it was brutal, too. The bottom line was that, if Will couldn't get his old fearlessness back, Islington would sell him on and he'd probably never wear an England shirt again.

Roy wracked his brain to think of a way he could help. He would get his friend tackling again if it was the last thing he did.

A WEEK LATER ROY found himself surprised to be inside Mel Park. It was his first time in the stands for months, the longest he'd ever not been there. With good reason. Mel Park had been a building site since the fire caused by its former owner, Barry 'the Meat' Cleaver. It was surrounded by wooden barriers and signs demanding you wear a hard hat if you went anywhere near it. And Roy was a stickler for the rules… most of the time.

But here he was. For the first game in the new stadium. A stadium that wasn't even finished yet, with scaffolding up around newly built stands and cherry pickers parked along the far end of the pitch, used for placing the sparkling new floodlights and advertising boards in place.

Roy felt weird. Conflicted. Envious. He wanted to be on the pitch. He remembered – before he was a footballer – that he would sneak into Mel Park and take in the stadium all alone, under the moonlight. He loved to be in here, whatever the circumstances were.

It was nice to be back.

But it was still weird. Weird, because this wasn't supposed to be his life anymore. Roy Race was meant to be out there on the pitch and not in the stands like he was now. And to make it all the harder it was his sister, Rocky, who was on the pitch, wearing the red and yellow of Melchester Rovers. Even more so because she was staring at him, grinning wildly. Roy watched her, knowing she had Roy's attention, as she then knelt on the pitch and kissed the turf.

He turned away, infuriated. Rocky did his head in. Every day she managed to get right under his skin. Only she could do this.

And the worst thing was that, however much she goaded him, he remained proud of her. Really proud. Here was his sister living the football dream she had had for years. He felt himself fill up with emotion at the idea, but still wishing she would let him be proud and not ruin it by winding him up.

'Ignore her,' Mum said, nudging Roy with her shoulder. 'It's just a more sophisticated way of stealing a sausage off your plate. She wants a reaction.'

'Ignore Rocky?' Roy replied. 'Easier said than done.'

Mum smiled and put her hand on Roy's knee. 'You're the most mild-mannered young man I know. Everyone thinks you're an angel. And you are an angel. Until Rocky pushes your buttons. Then you're a changed man. You are aware of that, Roy, aren't you?'

Roy nodded. He *was* aware and stared at the pitch just as the whistle went. And here he was, watching Rocky Race playing football in a Melchester Rovers strip for the first time. The team that had once been called Sowerby FC, based at the local sports centre, was now Melchester Rovers Women FC based at Mel Park.

The opposition – Barnley Women – kicked off and passed the ball so that one, two, three players could get a touch. Settling in. Except there really was no time to settle in. Because Rocky was on them before the ball was out of the centre circle. With a sliding tackle, she took the ball and it cannoned hard off a Barnley player and ballooned into touch.

'First touch by a Melchester Rovers Women's player in history goes to…'

'… Rocky Race,' Mum finished Roy's sentence.

Forgetting his irritation, Roy settled back to watch the game. He knew exactly where Rocky had got that move from. The brutal beginning to the Crowley game a few days before. Tackle them in the centre circle. Rocky was a proper student of the game.

There was a small crowd in. Four or five hundred fans who'd been allowed to return for the first game – a friendly – at the partially rebuilt Mel Park. That was how many they were allowed because of safety rules. Either way, it was good to be back in the ground where he had watched hundreds of games with his dad.

His dad. He was always thinking about his dad! There was nowhere Roy could go and nothing he could do and not think about him. Since Mum had alerted his consultant at the hospital about his new problems, Dad had had some more scans. Something was wrong. They all knew that. But they had to wait for the results. A few days of not knowing. A few days of living with the fear of something getting worse, or hoping that it wouldn't.

That was the problem when you had

someone in the family who was ill, Roy had learned over the last three years. You kind of had to live your normal life, be it college, work, going to the football, seeing mates, even day-to-day stuff at home. But the illness was always there.

Roy had imagined – when he was young and innocent – that if his mum or dad got ill the world would stop turning and they'd all sit around at home until the ill parent got better. But it wasn't like that. You just had to live with it. Life went on. There was no getting off. You had to go and watch your sister play football and be all supportive, while both of you were half-thinking about your ill dad. And, if you caught yourself *not* thinking about your ill dad, you felt guilty and rubbish.

Roy stopped staring at the empty stand on the far side of the pitch and went back to the game. A game where Melchester Rovers were on top. Easily. The opposition was defending deep and it was hard, really, for Rocky to influence the game.

'Patience,' Roy said under his breath, as Rocky snapped at opposition ankles to try and win the ball for her side.

When Rocky did get the ball – and had time to look up and choose a pass – Roy would always look up front. For Ffion, Sowerby's star striker. She should be back to the goal, calling in a pass, holding off a defender, then turning to attack.

Except she wasn't there, was she?

Roy looked at the sky above Mel Park. A deep blue turning black. He saw an aeroplane flying west. Maybe it was going to America. And if it was, maybe Ffion would see it land. She certainly wouldn't see it here.

Ffion Guthrie was not his girlfriend

anymore.

She was his ex.

She was on a footballing scholarship in the USA.

And that was it.

Back on the pitch, Roy saw Rocky beginning to run at players. Creating space. There was no opening up this Barnley defence. Not with long balls or short passes. Those moves always broke down. Now Rocky was running at them.

Powering past three tackles, she was fouled, but not before she slid a pass to the edge of the area and Melchester's right winger hammered the ball over the keeper and into the gaping net.

1–0 to Melchester Rovers.

It was 3–0 by half time. The players were applauded off the pitch, Rocky saluting Roy as she went under the stand.

Roy caught his mum staring at the hills beyond the stands. He put his arm round her and she looked at him.

Roy didn't say anything. What could you say?

He'll be okay...

It'll be fine...

Everything is going to work out...

Why would he say any of that when he feared that none of it was true? So he just held her for a moment then asked if she wanted a cup of tea.

Returning with a cup of tea and a Twix, Roy was surprised to see Penny Laine coming onto the pitch, followed by a crowd of photographers and journalists and a TV crew. Her shadow fell in four directions, created by floodlights across the lush green grass.

'Here we go,' Roy heard a voice behind them. 'PR Penny to the rescue.'

Roy smiled. Good nickname. He'd use that. But maybe not to her face.

'Welcome to Mel Park. I am Penny Laine, the new chairperson of Melchester Rovers Football Club. Welcome to Melchester Rovers Women's first ever game, I hope you're enjoying it as much as I am. Remember this day. Remember that you were here. Because it is the management's absolute ambition that Melchester Rovers Women will – within five years – become one of the top teams in Europe. We have already secured a place on the ladder to elite football with our training facilities. And with the help of one extra person, we will achieve our ambition.'

Roy noticed Serina Heracles standing on the touchline below.

Penny began again. 'With that in mind, we

would like to formally introduce to you the first manager of Melchester Rovers Women FC you. Former coach of the Dutch national side, please welcome Serina Heracles.'

Cameras flashed.

Applause poured off the stands.

Mouths smiled.

Amid all the sound and fury, Roy wondered about his sister. Would she be part of their plans for the new set up? It had sounded like it, the way Penny was saying she was going to build a team round Rocky. But would his sister be able to cope with professional football? That was what she had said she wanted. Years ago, as Roy walked her to school, she had asked him: Can you help me become a footballer?

So the answer was yes.

Wasn't it?

A FEW DAYS later, Roy and Rocky helped get Dad up, washed, breakfasted and into Mum's car, all before half-eight. Dad had an appointment at the hospital: the consultant had called to invite him and Mum in to get to the bottom of what was happening with Dad's tumour. Had it grown? Or was it still shrinking?

The atmosphere in the house was not good.

Barely anyone spoke and when they did it was in a cheerful voice that didn't match the vibe of the day. Roy had not let his mind drift into speculating what would happen if the test results weren't good. What did you do if a doctor told you that your dad was going to die soon? Because that was what was on the table. That was a possible outcome. Roy decided not to go there. He just kept helping, smiling and doing what Dad needed him to do to get ready.

Before she drove off, car keys jangling, Roy gave Mum a hug.

'Text me or call me if you need me. I can leave training.'

Mum nodded. 'If I need you, I will. Otherwise I'll see you at home after training. Rocky's got the afternoon off college.'

Mum looked briefly at Rocky, who was leaning in the doorway of their home. They waved at each other and smiled. But the smiles were strained. Not like normal smiles at all. But this wasn't a normal day.

Roy stood in the road after the car had

gone. He watched the indicator go, then saw the blue Honda Civic ease into the traffic on the main road at the bottom of their terraced street.

He glanced at his sister and they stared at each other wordlessly before she disappeared into the house.

'Training,' Roy said aloud to himself.

He needed to get his football head on.

BACK AT MEL Park, Roy was enjoying being on the pitches. The squad were performing short fast passing drills. They worked in fours, two against two, one pair trying to get the ball off the other, enclosed within a marked area, five metres by five.

Roy and Asif trying to win the ball off Will and Lofty. Then vice versa.

Roy was pretty sure that Johnny Dexter

had them doing this to try to help Will get his tackling mojo back. But it wasn't working. Every time Roy went in to challenge Will for the ball, his friend pulled out, or just didn't give it 100%.

Roy tried to push things, in an attempt to draw Will into a tackle. He wanted to force his friend to challenge himself. But how? How do you tell someone they've got a weakness and you're all over it?

When they took drinks before moving on to do some warm-down exercises, Will nudged into Roy.

'How's your dad?'

'Fine.'

'Really?'

'Yeah, fine.' Roy wanted to change the subject. He didn't want to think about his dad and mum sat, holding hands, staring across a desk in the consultant's office, being told...

No.

Not that.

No thoughts about that. This was work, not home. Roy switched subjects.

'So... about your tackling... what's going on, Will? You're not at the races.'

There. He'd said it.

Will hung his head. 'I've lost it, mate,' he said.

'Then you'll have to get it back.'

'Easier said than done,' Will laughed bleakly.

Roy frowned. He was going to solve this. He was glad to have a problem, a challenge. He might not be able to help himself and his own family, but he could help Will.

But how?

Before he could think about it anymore, they heard sudden and angry shouting coming across the pitch. Roy and Will turned to see

Nat Gosden standing over Jimmy Slade. Jimmy was lying on the ground, laughing, until Gosden leaned down to grab the younger player by his collar and drag him up onto his feet.

It was kicking off. Big time.

Roy, the first to react, sprinted over to stand in between the two midfielders, taking a punch to his shoulder, as Slade began to fight back against Gosden.

As the blow hit him, Roy felt an explosion of something inside his head. Rage. Grief. Anger. He had no idea what it was called. But it was there. His heart was hammering. He felt like he could tear the turf off the pitch and rip it to pieces. Like he could put everyone on that training field down and leave them there.

'Back off, both of you,' he shouted at Nat and Jimmy, shoving them both away, hearing the echo of his words coming back off the railway bridge two or three hundred yards away. It was then he noticed he'd somehow pushed both Gosden and Slade to the ground.

Silence. Apart from the croak of a crow flapping above the training fields. Then Slade started laughing.

'What was that? Are you the Incredible Hulk or something?' Jimmy said, as Patrick Nolan helped him up and Nat Gosden, glowering, got to his feet.

Roy was standing between Nat and Jimmy.

'I can be if I have to,' Roy growled. 'You two need to go for a coffee after training and sort this out. I want unity in this fami… I mean team.' Roy felt his voice go, like his throat was closing up. But he pushed on. 'We need to fight together, not against each other. Do you hear me?'

Silence again.

'Sorry, Roy,' Nat said.

Then Jimmy said the same. 'Yeah. Sorry, mate. We will.'

And Roy understood everything in that moment. They knew. The whole Melchester Rovers squad knew what was going on at home. And that they were willing to stop fighting each other to make him calm down, feel better.

'Coffee? After training?' Roy said, his energy draining away.

He saw Nat frown, still reluctant.

'Or I go upstairs. As captain. Let Penny Laine sort you out. Maybe send you both out on loan to some dump down south?'

'Coffee?' Nat conceded, glancing at Jimmy.

'So long as I can have a choccy muffin, Dad,' Jimmy joked.

Another silence. Roy knew it was remarks like that from Jimmy that did Nat's head in. But he noted that Nat didn't react, so he clapped the older player on the shoulder. Then stared across the training ground. The wave of emotion that had brought his anger on was turning into just emotion now. He had to get away from everyone. Alone. He could deal with things alone.

'I need a run,' he muttered, then ignoring anything else being said, went off, alone, to do laps of the pitch, dribbling a ball in front of him.

He ran – head down – for a half lap, his mind going over and over what he'd do when he pulled out his phone back in the changing room. Wait for a text? Call Mum? Find out the news? Round and round went his thoughts as he punted the ball ahead of him, left foot, right foot, left foot, right foot. He had never felt so alone.

Until he heard footsteps behind him. Roy glanced over his shoulder and saw immediately that he was being flanked in silence by Will on one side and Lofty on the other. And that – behind them – the rest of the squad were running too. Even Gosden and Slade, shoulder to shoulder. Ten yards behind them. But with him.

And Roy understood that although he was on his own, he wasn't alone.

15

ROY WALKED HOME, striding up the hill to stretch his legs out after training. He liked this about his life. Yes, he had to eat steamed fish and steamed vegetables, but he could still walk about his home town without being hassled.

Nearly home, in front of the mini-market on the corner, he saw Rocky. She was sitting on the wall, eating a bag of sweets. For a moment Roy thought she'd been home, heard bad news about Dad and had come out to get away and find a sugar rush. Then he saw she still had her college bag.

She'd not been home. Not yet. She'd stopped for sweets. Maybe she was waiting for him?

Roy was about to say: 'You'll have to give sweets up now you're going to be an elite player.' But he didn't. He just put his hand out like he would have when he and Rocky were six and eight. And Rocky dropped three or four Haribos into his hand.

'Not been home?'

'No.'

'Waiting for me?'

Rocky nodded and slid off the wall.

'Come on,' she said.

Brother and sister walked up the terraced street together. A sudden shower of rain seemed to spill off the moor behind their houses to soak them. Neither of them flinched from the cloudburst.

Mum's car was in front of their house.

Roy put his hand on the door handle and froze. He couldn't turn it. He looked into his sister's eyes. She looked back. This felt like one of those moments in your life when you reach a forked path and you know things are about to change.

'It might be okay,' Rocky told him.

Roy pulled the handle down, opened the door and called out: 'We're home.'

Roy could see Dad down the hallway, through the kitchen door. He was sitting in his wheelchair. He was trying to smile.

Rocky rushed ahead of Roy to hug her dad. Roy saw Dad studying him over Rocky's shoulder as he came into the room. Then Mum was there. She smiled a greeting, then stepped to the side.

Her eyes were swollen. The kettle was boiling. There was a cat on the back wall staring at Roy. And Mum said: 'It's not good news, kids. Sit down.'

THEY SAT AROUND the kitchen table. Mum talking. Roy and Rocky listening. Dad watching.

'The brain tumour is growing again,' Mum explained. 'And – as we know – it's inoperable. They also told us that the cancer has spread.'

'In your brain?' Rocky asked.

Dad shook his head.

'Where to, then?' Rocky asked.

Roy sat in his chair, looking out of the kitchen window. He couldn't think, let alone speak. He was glad Rocky could. The cat had disappeared.

'Everywhere,' Mum said, putting her hand on Dad's hand.

'So what does that mean?' Rocky asked.

'It means that... the truth is...' Roy heard his mum swallow, 'that your father has four to six weeks left with us and that for the next week or two he'll be up and about, but then he won't.'

Dad lifted his other hand – the one he could lift. He put it across the table so that both Roy and Rocky could put their hand on his.

Mum cleared her throat.

'This will not be easy. But we've coped with the last few years, so I know we can cope with the next few weeks. We are strong. Each of us and all of us.'

Roy's mind flitted to the dressing room. Mum sounded like Johnny Dexter doing a team talk.

'Just tell us what we can do,' Roy said.

'Same as usual,' Mum said. 'Keep doing what you're doing. You're both amazing. And let's keep talking.'

'Okay,' Roy and Rocky said together.

'Any questions?' Mum asked.

Roy and Rocky shook their heads. There were questions. Lots of them. But they could wait.

'Right,' Mum said, standing. 'Your dad's tired and so am I. We're going to bed for a rest.'

AFTER ROY HAD helped Dad to bed, chatting to him about training, narrating the fight between Nat and Jimmy, but playing down his own role, Roy and Rocky found themselves sitting in the front room.

At first in complete silence.

Roy studied the closed curtains. The wheelchair that sat at the end of the sofa. All his FIFA stuff on the floor. The stain in the carpet where he'd spilt that can of Coke, when he used to drink Coke. But not anymore: the club made him write down everything he ate and drank and told him what he could and couldn't have. They tested him to make sure his sugar levels were right.

'Six to four weeks,' Rocky said at last, breaking into Roy's work-thinking.

Roy nodded.

'It's nothing,' Rocky went on.

'I know.'

They listened to Mum's voice in the room above. The soft sound of her reading a book to Dad.

'Do you remember when she used to read to us?' Roy asked, glancing at the full cup of cold tea in front of him.

Rocky laughed, briefly. 'She's not doing silly voices for *him*.'

Brother and sister found themselves laughing.

Then crying.

Until Rocky left the room.

Now that he was alone, he flicked on

FIFA. He picked up the controller and began to play. Melchester Rovers versus Tynecaster United. FA Cup quarter final. He played with the sound off, so he could hear Mum reading still.

2–0 down within a few minutes, Roy paused the game. There was no way he was going to win this. Not in this mood.

He stood up. The walls and the furniture seemed to be closing in on him as he did so. Like that scene in *Star Wars* when the sides of the room are moving in to crush some of the characters. He felt like that.

Normally – at a time like this – Roy would go for a run. But that was before this new regime at Rovers.

Rest.

That's what he had to do after training. No other games of football. No five-a-side with mates. No running. No climbing ladders.

No using chainsaws, drills, floor sanders. He had signed a contract to promise that all he would do was walk. He was allowed to walk.

Roy put his head round the kitchen door. Rocky was there staring at her phone.

'I'm off for a walk,' Roy said.

'Fine.' His sister didn't look up.

'Want to come?'

'No.'

Roy smiled. Rocky was in monosyllabic mode.

'Tell Mum to text me if she needs me.'

'Yeah.'

Roy grabbed his coat and made for the front door.

Outside, the streets were deserted. The sun had gone down and all that was left was grey skies, fading light and rain and a wind whipping off the moor nudging wheelie bins down the road, singing in the telephone wires.

Roy walked up the hill towards the moor. He didn't mind weather like this. As long as he was wrapped up – as his mum used to say – he enjoyed rain and wind on his face. And the wind was strong, almost pushing him up towards the moor. It was like it wanted him here. Sometimes he felt like that about the moor. That it had a mind of its own. That it cared about him. Or that he was a part of it, or it of him. Either way, it was a special place to him. And the bonus was that weather like this meant no one else would be out on the moor. He would have it to himself.

There were some disadvantages to being a professional footballer. You couldn't do the exercise you wanted to do. You weren't supposed to eat sweets. And people would want to talk to you – about the game. About your fame. And Roy was fine with that. The fans paid his wages, gave him their support. Why wouldn't he chat to them? He was one of them, after all.

But on a day like this – with news like that – Roy was thankful for the wild weather. The idea that the moor had brought bad weather to help him that evening crossed his mind. Roy smiled. Why not? Maybe such things happened. Maybe when it was bad weather and everybody was moaning about it, the wind and rain meant someone else was able to walk on the moor to be alone to think.

And another thing he liked was that – when it was wild, the wind pounding at him, rain thrashing him – he felt calm inside. He had always liked this: he could find a deep calm inside himself when it was wild outside.

Roy walked across the football pitches to the edge of the moor, where he'd be able to look down across the city. He skirted the woods and found some shelter out of the wind and rain behind the prefabricated changing rooms.

He sat on the step and, although he could hear the wind and rain, here he was dry and unaffected.

When his phone vibrated, he stood up, ready to head home. Maybe Mum needed him. Then he looked at his screen and saw a text and sat down.

Ffion.

Facetime

What was this? Was the universe arranging text messages for him now?

Roy called Ffion, then held his phone in front of him, so he could see her face.

And there she was. Her red hair pulled back

in a ponytail. It surprised Roy. She looked different. Was it her hair? Her voice? He didn't know. But she looked more American every time he saw her. Whatever that meant.

'You're on the moor,' she smiled.

'Yeah. Out for a walk.'

Ffion hesitated. Was she reading him? Picking up on his facial expression? His body language? He felt like he was being scanned at an airport.

'What's up?' she said at last.

Roy shrugged. 'Stuff,' he managed to say. 'How's America?'

'Forget America. Talk to me.'

Roy was ready to explain Dad's new diagnosis. He had all the words ready.

'Dad saw the specialist today and…'

Now Roy found he couldn't speak. He wanted to say *Dad got his results today. From his consultant. He's a lot worse. He's been given four weeks to live. That's it. Mum's reading to him. He's very tired. It's kind of like he's not there, but hidden away inside himself. He's not said anything for days.*

But he said nothing. He just stared at Ffion's face staring back at his. Then she began to speak to him.

'Vic told me something was going on. Then Rocky texted me. She told me. About the diagnosis. I'm so sorry, Roy. I wish I was there and could hug you and tell you face to face. And I wish I'd never come to America. I should be there with you and…'

'Stop,' Roy said.

Ffion stopped.

Roy wanted Ffion back more than anything, but he had to tell her otherwise.

'I need you to be *there*. I need to know you are doing something so amazing. Every day – even though I miss you – your being there living your dream is one of the things that makes me happy. So please don't think that.'

Roy saw Ffion smile. She looked relieved. Like she had heard what she wanted to hear. Ffion didn't want to come home. She was loving her life. And Roy wanted to support that 100%, even though he was desperate for her to put her arms around him and hold him. He knew she and he were over. They were friends now: that was all.

Roy's mind turned for something to speak to her about.

'Don't tell Vic,' he said. 'About Dad. I want to keep it to myself for now. People act weird at the club. I want them to act normal. I need work to be normal. I reckon I can cope if work is normal.'

Ffion didn't say anything back. And Roy knew.

'You've told him already?'

Ffion nodded. 'I'm sorry.'

'Well, can you tell him to keep his gob shut?'

'I'll try,' Ffion said.

'Thanks,' Roy said. 'Now, tell me about your life. I'm sick of mine.'

Roy slipped out of the front door before anyone else was up. Rovers had an early training session ahead of a game the following day. He'd decided to get out early, walk into work and have his breakfast there, so that he didn't wake Mum and Dad, who were planning to lie in. And the breakfasts at Mel Park were spot on.

There was a vehicle parked next to Mum's outside the house, its engine going.

Vic's Land Rover.

Unmistakable. The only one in town.

An ex-Army Desert Land Rover, shades

of yellowy sandy brown. A vehicle that had – according to the woman who sold it to Vic – seen action in Iraq. For some reason Vic had named the Land Rover Roy.

Last season Vic had struggled with his mental health. Anger. Self-loathing. He'd been on the edge. But – with the help of Roy, his sister Ffion and the club – Vic had been to counselling and come out the other side a stronger man.

'Lift?' Vic shouted out of the window.

Roy didn't want a lift, but he didn't want to be rude to his co-captain either. So he jumped in and fastened his seat belt. The Land Rover's vibrating engine and oily smell made Roy feel slightly sick. That and his empty stomach.

Vic indicated, and Roy (the Land Rover) moved off, the veteran engine vibrating so much Roy couldn't hear what Vic was saying.

'Yeah?'

'I love you, but...'

'What?'

'What I need from you...'

'Is?'

Roy decided to be direct. To spell it out.

'You to be my teammate. I need someone to play football with who won't ask me about my dad or make sad faces at me to show me he's thinking about me.'

'What?' he shouted back.

'I said Ffion told me,' Vic yelled. 'About your dad.'

Roy nodded. 'Right,' he said.

'What?' Vic yelled.

'I said… I… I asked her not to tell anyone.'

Vic grinned. 'But I'm not anyone. I'm Vic!'

Vic slowed down, parked outside Lidl and cut the engine.

'So, I'm here, brother,' he went on, quieter. 'To listen. Do you want to talk?'

'I don't.'

Vic put his hands together as if he was praying. This was another part of New Vic. He used to be all rage and outrage. Now he was calm, meditative, priest-like.

'When you're ready,' he pressed, 'I'm here. For whatever you need from me, brother.'

'Vic?'

Vic nodded. 'Okay, brother. That's it then. But, when you need me... you know... I'm here.'

Roy said thank you and turned to look at the next lane of traffic so Vic couldn't see him smile.

AFTER AN EASY breakfast with Vic, Will and Asif, Roy looked up to see that pretty much the whole team was in the club canteen, eating porridge, bananas, poached egg on toast, drinking one of half a dozen different flavoured juices on offer. It was like every team member was there. Except Nat Gosden.

Roy was just about to lean in to Will to praise the club's new owners for putting on such healthy food and motivating the squad to eat well, when he saw Lofty in the doorway, staring directly at him.

'Come and see this,' Lofty said.

'See what?'

'They've opened up the main stand. The reception area. You can go inside.'

Now the whole team were on their feet, keen to see. But Roy was delighted that every one of them cleared their place, took their crockery and cutlery over to the kitchen, and put it in the dishwasher. This was part of the team ethos that Mouse and Dexter were trying to form. Everyone looks out for everyone. From the kitchens to the pitches to the matchday stewards. They were one. They were Melchester Rovers.

The young Melchester Rovers footballers walked across the car park tarmac to the main stand. It looked brilliant. Huge sheets of plate glass. The words of the club motto – *Work Hard, Win Well* – in stone above the door. Then through sliding glass to a sparkling, well-lit reception area with sofas and a long wooden reception desk. On the walls were images of the club's fans, of the new stadium, the new sponsor's logos.

'This is Mel Rovers,' Patrick Nolan grinned. 'This is our future.'

Roy felt his eyebrows crinkle before he understood something was missing.

What was it?

What was gone?

Then he understood.

All the pictures of the old players were no longer there. The generation of Melchester Rovers legends who had won the league multiple times, the European cup, the rest. Even the internationals board – which listed all of Melchester Rovers' internationals through history – had been replaced.

All of it. The players and history from

his dad's era. Gone.

The wave of sadness that hit him was a shock. Like he was frozen to the spot, speechless with rage. All he could think of was his dad seeing this; then he had to stop thinking.

He said nothing, then wandered outside to get some air, to hide his feelings. Why did everything have to bring him back to Dad? Outside, skirting the club car park, Roy saw Fred and his dog, Rover.

Fred was Roy's favourite Rovers fan. After his dad.

There it was again. Dad. Dad. Dad. Dad. Dad. Dad. Dad.

'Alright, Fred,' Roy said. 'How's the dog?'

'He's fine.' Fred studied Roy, then grimaced. 'You've not heard, have you?'

'Heard what?' Roy tensed, his mind

unravelling along the canal and up his street to the room where his dad would be in bed. Worse? Better? Had something happened?

'Gosden,' Fred said. 'He's been shipped out. On loan. To Huddersfool Town.'

Roy felt his eyes widen, then he turned and saw Penny Laine on the first floor, inside her office, looking down at him.

'By her,' Fred said, following his line of sight.

Penny Laine. Who was this woman? Shipping out players without a word? Taking the pictures of Melchester legends off the walls? It was too much.

Midday. Saturday afternoon. Melchester Rovers versus Tonmouth FC. At Tynecaster United's Tayir Stadium.

A home game, but these games never really felt like home games. Roy yearned for the day he and his teammates could jog onto Mel Park once again. He was still deeply envious of his sister, already allowed to play on the hallowed turf. But enough of emotions like envy and yearning. There was football to be played. And, at least they had the home dressing room to themselves today.

The TV cameras were in town to offer

live coverage to the UK and a hundred other countries round the world. To watch two mid-table second-tier English teams battling it out to see which could finish the day in the top half of the table, not the bottom. A win and Rovers would be five points from the play-off places, and three points further away from the relegation zone. A defeat and relegation fear might start to work its way into the team psyche.

A big game. Every game was big. But what was it about today that didn't feel right? Maybe the dressing room with two new players in there: Will and Slade? Maybe the fact that Nat Gosden had been sent away without a word from the owners? Roy had sensed an unspoken anger – even blame – towards Jimmy Slade for what had happened to Nat Gosden. Nat – after some teething problems – had been a great role model to them all. Was this what it felt like at a club that was having problems behind the scenes? Was this the price of success? The club became more ruthless?

Maybe. But Roy needed to focus. Because it wasn't just the team that was off. He was too. His passes. His focus on opposition players. It just didn't feel right.

Roy thought Mouse got it spot on with his team talk.

'A football team changes year on year, month on month, week on week. Players come, like Jimmy, here. And players go, like Paco at the start of the season. Sometimes they even go and come back.'

The manager's remark led to smiles. And a couple of the players ruffled Will's hair.

'But we are a team. We are a group of players. And so long as we play the Melchester Rovers way, so long as we support every teammate for ninety-plus minutes, we will be going in the right direction and we'll have a good day. Got me?'

'Got you, gaffer,' the players all said in unison.

But – even so – today was not that kind of day.

TEN MINUTES IN Roy, back to goal, holding the ball up, underplayed a ball wide to Will to see it cut out easily by the opposition, leading to a rapid counterattack from Tonmouth and a shot skimming the top of Gordon Stewart's goal.

It was a warning. And Roy knew it was his fault. You give the ball away against a decent team and they'll use pace and accurate passing to cut you into ribbons.

He had to lead by example. That was

Roy's job, wasn't it? He was the captain. He had to be at his best and play at a standard that his teammates could follow. He needed to be more careful. More clinical.

The first proper break in play came after twenty minutes – an injury to the Tonmouth central defender, a huge guy who Roy had already nicknamed 'the Beast'. Roy used the opportunity to get the team in a huddle. He wanted to fire them up. Change the mindset.

'We have to forget what's happened off the pitch. The next seventy minutes are everything,' he said.

Roy's words didn't work. All he got was funny looks. It was like his teammates were wanting to ask him: What's gone on off the pitch? What do we need to worry about?

He saw Jimmy Slade shake his head, like he disagreed, but he didn't say anything. Roy was glad Slade hadn't voiced his concerns.

But – deep down – Roy knew he'd misjudged it as the game moved on into the second quarter. It was quite possible that the other players weren't that bothered about Nat Gosden. They didn't mind that all the club's past had been taken off the walls: they were interested in the future.

Things got worse as the first half moved on. Passes were going astray. Into touch. You could sense the unease in the crowd now.

They couldn't understand how a normally fluent, confident group were having such a bad day at the office. Neither could Roy.

Then things got worse.

In the thirty-seventh minute Lofty slid in to make a rash tackle in the area.

Penalty.

Red card.

The spot kick buried by the opposition striker.

0–1.

How were Melchester Rovers going to come back from this? How could Roy fix it so that they got their mojo back? Were they destined for another defeat and then the slippery slope into the relegation zone?

Roy DROPPED BACK into midfield for the restart, now they were down to ten men, leaving Will alone up front. But Will was still avoiding tackles. They wouldn't score many today if this was going to be the pattern of the game. The only player who seemed to be in the zone – or giving it 100% – was Jimmy Slade.

Even Dexter's half-time rant wasn't enough to stimulate any change.

'What's going on, lads?'

'It's tough out there,' Roy admitted. 'Just feels weird. But the second half is a fresh start. We're only one down. We can win this. Tonmouth have their weaknesses.'

The conversation went on. They spent the rest of the half-time break studying the opposition's weaknesses to make the second half different.

Until Johnny Dexter stood up.

'Lads?' he said. 'I want you to imagine yourself in the Tonmouth dressing room. I have and I can tell you exactly what they're going to be thinking. They'll be considering two outcomes.

'One, they have an extra man, it shows and they steamroller us, coming off the pitch grateful we were down to ten men. 'Two, they are frustrated and come off the pitch wondering why it is that sometimes, when you play a team down to ten men, it's even harder than when they had eleven.

'I know you, lads. And I know you will

do everything to make sure it's the latter. Okay?'

BUT THE SECOND half was the same. Just the same. Roy heard a voice on the pitch. Just as the crowd went quiet. The words echoed around the unease of Mel Park.

'Get forward. This is pathetic. You're not giving me anything.'

Jimmy Slade had said it. Roy felt cross. Who was Slade to boss the others around on his debut?

But – deep down in his football brain – Roy knew Slade was right. This was about the team, not individual players. Hadn't Penny Laine said something like that?

'Come on,' Roy yelled. 'Slade's right. We fight. We win every ball. We can turn this round play by play.'

Roy focused on every pass. Every tackle. Making it as good as he could. He gave it everything. Led by example. And he could see that his teammates were doing the same. Piece by piece rebuilding their game.

But still, up front, Will wasn't getting the message.

Rovers would win the ball, keep possession, push forward into the final third, then Will – front man and target man – would pull out of the key challenge. Exposed, on his own up front, Will's tackle-shyness was obvious to everyone.

Jimmy sidled up to Roy.

'Swap with him. You go up front. He can play deeper.'

Roy considered it for a second. Then he shook his head. 'But this is where the tackles are. I'm better here. And, anyway, that's the boss's call.'

'Just do it,' Jimmy grinned. 'They might thank you.'

Roy shook his head again. He would never do that. Snapping out of the conversation, Roy noticed a new chant from the crowd.

'One Will Gray. There's only one Will Gray. There's only one Will Graaaaaaaaaaaaayyyyy,' rolling down the stands.

Roy punched the air and roared. 'Come on!'

That's what they needed. Support. That's what Will needed. All those drills Roy had tried with him. They'd not worked. But maybe, just maybe, the Melchester faithful could put some fire in his belly.

The game moved on. The clock ran down. And down.

Fifteen minutes to go.

Ten minutes to go.

Five, four, three...

Roy played deeper and deeper into midfield, more and more desperate to get the ball and play it up field, doing the opposite of what Jimmy Slade had suggested and wondering if Jimmy had been right all along.

As time ran down to one minute of injury time remaining, Roy won the ball deep again. Then he looked up for a second. Because a second was all you have. Once you've won the ball against a team 1–0 up with minutes to go, you're going to be tackled. Fast.

Roy saw Will facing him, then peel away from his man, running in a diagonal, pointing ahead of him, asking for the pass. And, in the split second it took to decide, Roy saw something in Will's eyes. Something fierce. The crowd had lifted him. This was it.

Roy slid the ball across the grass, dissecting the Tonbridge midfield, then, as he ran on, he saw Will and the big defender – the Beast

– chasing for the ball. One on one. Shoulder to shoulder. Now the volume of the crowd lifted even more and Will went in, taking the ball first, then the man, the two players in a tangle of legs and arms.

Will had won the tackle. Against the Beast.

The roar from the crowd was like pure adrenaline to Roy. He felt power surge up his back, through his limbs. And now, as he sprinted towards goal, the ball span out to him. Perfect. Perfect luck! He took one touch to stop the ball spinning, easing it to his left, then he hit it.

Hard. Straight.

Past the keeper. Between the posts. And into the net.

Goal.

1–1.

Awesome.

And as Will came over to congratulate Roy, the crowd was chanting again.

'ONE WILL GRAY!' was cascading round Mel Park. And Roy was thrilled. The Melchester faithful knew what was going on. Will had beaten his fear of the tackle. He was back. They were praising him and not

Roy, the goal scorer.

Roy was as proud of his friend as he was of the club's fans. And he knew that, although they'd dropped points today, they had their front man back for the rest of the season.

With Dad resting upstairs, the three of them sat at the kitchen table in silence. Mum drinking tea. Roy, water. Rocky, a can of Coke.

Roy eyed the Coke, wishing he could have one too. Rocky pushed it across the table.

'Have it,' she said.

Roy shook his head. 'Not allowed.'

Rocky shrugged. And Roy wished he wasn't a professional footballer so that he could eat fish fingers and drink Coke.

But he was a stickler for rules. They all knew that.

As they descended into silence again, because none of them was quite sure what to say, Roy had a terrible understanding that this was how things were going to be every day soon. This kitchen and its worktops, the window with the blind that wouldn't come all the way down anymore and the table where they'd eaten every meal for years. But three of them. Not four.

He realised that they might never have the four of them sitting round the table again. That Dad might never come into the kitchen again. Or come down the stairs. He certainly wasn't capable of that today.

It was hard to even imagine, let alone understand.

It was dark outside. The air near the kitchen window felt chilled. Autumn was coming. Then winter.

'We have a few weeks with your dad,'

Mum said bluntly. 'And we have to make some decisions.'

Neither Roy nor Rocky said anything. How could you reply to that?

'I have been giving it some thought, and I think, this week, Dad can get out for a trip. A last trip. After this week he won't be well enough. That is what the consultant said to me.'

Roy could see where Mum was going. He didn't interrupt her.

'You each have a home game in the next week. Rocky on Saturday. Roy in the middle of next week. I think your dad can only manage one.'

Roy felt a sudden bolt of terror. He could barely control himself. He stood up and went to fill his glass of water again. Just to move. Just to not have to sit there and think about his dad in the crowd watching him playing for the last time. The idea terrified him. So much he was shocked.

He heard Rocky say: 'He can watch Roy. It's fine.'

Roy kept his back turned from his mum and sister. His chest was convulsing. He struggled to breathe. Then – without turning to face them – he shook his head.

'I don't think I can,' he said.

'Can what?' Mum's soft voice.

'Play in front of Dad. I don't think I can do it again.'

Now Roy struggled not only to breathe, but to stay on his feet. What was happening to him?

Next, he felt arms around him. His sister's. They guided him into a chair and he put his head on the table. But not before he caught his red-faced reflection in the window onto the night, that cat staring back at him. He didn't want them to see him crying. He didn't want anyone to see him crying. He hated crying.

With his mum's arm round him now, he took a deep breath in then out, then sat up to face his sister.

'He should go to Mel Park. To see you. We can't make him go to the Tayir for his...'

Roy didn't say the rest. He was learning

that you could say half sentences and his mum and sister knew what he meant. And that was good because there were some sentences he really didn't want to say in full.

THERE WERE TWO thousand fans in for Melchester Rovers Women's second game at Mel Park. News had got out that you could watch this new team and fans were beginning to flock to see them, keen to support any team they possibly could in the red and yellow of Rovers at Mel Park.

People were talking about the team on social media. The main theme was that it was great to have two Melchester Rovers teams to support now. More chances to watch football being played in red and yellow.

The ground sounded weird as the voices

of a smaller number of fans bounced off the empty unfinished stands on the other side of the pitch.

'One day Mel Park will be full to watch Rocky and the team,' Roy said to Dad, nudging him.

Dad nudged Roy back, shoulder to shoulder, father to son.

Dad had so few words now. His illness – and the operation that followed his diagnosis – had taken away his ability to speak. For a year or two he had managed a few words. But now, none. Not a word for eight or nine weeks. The tumour in his dad's brain was growing. As it grew it stopped parts of Dad's brain working and so stopped parts of his body working too.

His arms.

His legs.

His voice.

But he could still smile. And he'd been smiling a lot as he and Roy watched from the track pitch side, where they'd been allowed to park Dad's wheelchair.

Smiling, because Rocky was bossing another game. She was becoming more and more the midfield enforcer. The tough player. The one players in the other team did not want to tackle, would not want to play near.

'She's stronger now,' Roy said. 'Look at her. She's wearing the colours on the pitch at Mel Park and bossing the game.'

They both watched as Rocky won the ball in a midfield tussle and forced her way through two tackles to set up a goal.

The cheer of the Melchester Rovers fans echoed around the stands and Roy saw Rocky, hands on hips, breathing heavily and watching him and Dad.

Roy put two thumbs up. One for him. One for Dad.

Then Rocky was back in the game, closing opposition players down, forcing them to pass back to the defence. Any game plan that this team from over the Pennines had come with seemed to be in shreds as they were constantly hassled by Rocky and her teammates.

The new manager – Heracles – was pacing up and down the track, calling out orders in her strong Dutch accent. She had a reputation for playing a pressing game. And it was showing already. The perfect style of play for Rocky, Roy thought.

'I don't know how she's done this. But they're already a better team. Don't you think, Dad?' Roy asked, hoping to surprise Dad into replying.

Dad nudged Roy and smiled and for a moment Roy thought how mad it was that this was the last time Dad would come for a day out, probably. And yet here they were having a normal conversation about football, side by side, watching a game at Mel Park. Like they always had. Since Roy was tiny. This was their thing. The football. Watching football at Mel Park. And Roy was so happy that he had said he thought this should be the game Dad came to, not his. Because – even though he knew his dad was proud he played for Rovers – he knew that this, them together, watching the game, meant more.

'You know,' Roy said. 'This is so good. We've been coming to the football for years, you and me. Then it stopped because I was on the pitch, not sat next to you. And now…' Roy felt his throat tighten. 'And now we're here again. You and me. Dad… I've missed this.'

Roy couldn't speak anymore. He felt his dad's left hand drop onto Roy's right hand. Dad agreed. That meant the world.

And – for the first time since they'd heard the catastrophic news about Dad – Roy felt okay. He knew this moment would live in his memory for the rest of his life.

Now the whistle for half time went and – as she had for the last game – Penny Laine strode onto the pitch with a microphone and a camerawoman tracking her every move.

'Another announcement from PR Penny,' Roy joked to Dad. 'What now?'

PENNY WAS FOLLOWED onto the pitch at Mel Park with a camerawoman, a lighting person and a sound recordist as well as another woman carrying a clipboard and a small box about the size of a shoebox.

'Time for another speech from our glorious leader,' Roy muttered to Dad. He'd now told Dad about Nat and Jimmy and how she'd taken the pictures off the walls. It was clear to Roy that both outcomes troubled Dad.

'We stand here, this afternoon, on the pitch in a nearly rebuilt Mel Park,' Penny began, pausing for a cheer from the fans as she appeared to study the new stands, the remaining scaffolding and cherry picker at the far end of the mostly empty stadium. 'I am thrilled to say that – very soon – this stadium will be full again, as we move from our temporary stadium back to our home.'

Another cheer from the stands as Roy's mind began running through the fixtures coming up that month. Which game did she mean? Very soon? Did that mean Dad could come and watch him here one last time? Maybe that would be okay. Maybe he'd like it.

'So today seems a fitting time and place – as we take a break in enjoying Melchester Rovers Women play – to announce what I hope will make Melchester Rovers a football club to be admired and copied across the world.'

Roy looked at Dad. Dad at Roy.

'What's this?' Roy asked Dad.

Dad shrugged.

Penny Laine went on to explain. 'My father and I – as custodians of Melchester Rovers Football Club – are delighted to announce that we are now ready to give the club to the fans. And it begins tonight.'

Penny paused. Roy could hear a hubbub of muttering from the crowd. As he listened, Roy watched Penny carefully and saw she was waiting for that reaction.

She was good at this. Good at playing a crowd.

'Over the next few weeks we are going to gift shares in Melchester Rovers to all season ticket holders and members. The fans will hold one hundred per cent of the club's value in those shares. Shares will stay in the family of the recipient, handed down from mother to daughter, and...' Penny glanced at

Roy and his dad on the touchline '... from father to son. These new owners – the loyal fanbase of this club – will make all decisions about the running of the club. I will remain the chairperson for as long as the new owners want me here. In doing this we hope – as I have said before – to make Melchester Rovers more like Atletico Cervantes and Borussia Goethe. And tonight we shall give the first of those shares to the first of our supporters. But it will be something we do in private. It is not for the cameras. It is for a fan we want to recognise as our best.'

Slowly and steadily applause built and built in the stands, then the cheering began.

This was a moment of history. Roy felt tears in his eyes. What was this? He couldn't believe it. He looked at Dad, who was clapping his working hand against his paralysed hand and gazing lovingly at Roy.

'This is your club,' Penny cried out. 'Your city. Your future. A new model for football in the twenty-first century.'

After the applause and after Penny had come off the pitch, Roy saw Kevin Mouse and Johnny Dexter walking along the touchline with the small wooden box that Penny must have handed to them after her speech. She was standing watching them now, from a distance.

'Danny. Roy. We have something for you.'
Johnny was speaking. Roy could sense his
voice was straining. He had never heard him
like this before.

They handed Dad a box. Dad used his
good hand to flip it open to find a scroll of
paper, wrapped with a ribbon.

Roy yearned to help, but he didn't. If Dad
wanted help he'd let him know. Dad deftly
took the ribbon off the scroll and unfurled
the piece of paper.

It was a bond. Shares in the club. The
reference number was 00001.

'It's the first one. For you, Danny. For
services rendered to Melchester Rovers.'

Dad nodded and his eyes filled up.

Roy could barely breathe, he was so
overwhelmed: the club were giving his dad
the first fans' share in Melchester Rovers.

Dad nodded, smiling.

Mouse and Johnny shook Dad's hand.

Roy glanced down the track to see Penny was watching. She looked away quickly.

'Listen, gaffer,' Roy said. 'Can you stay with Dad for a minute? I need to talk to Penny.'

Mouse nodded. 'My pleasure.'

'Go easy,' Johnny cautioned.

Roy didn't know what he was going to say to her, but he would go easy. He always did, didn't he? But he couldn't deny that there was a lot going through his mind.

Gosden being shipped out.

Letting Slade keep his place.

Taking the pictures down of the players from the past.

All things that really vexed Roy.

Then this. Giving the football club to the fans. Giving the first share to Dad. Why Dad?

Penny saw Roy approaching and waited

by the players' tunnel, her head up, watching him. Neither smiling, nor frowning. A ripple of applause followed Roy as he walked along the bottom of the stand. He applauded back, arms in the air, paying respect to the fans.

'Roy? How are you?' Penny said.

'Good. I just... I just wanted to say thanks. For that thing you did. With Dad. And there's some other stuff I want to talk to you about.'

It all came out in a flush of words. Roy wasn't even sure if he was making sense. As he spoke Roy looked in Penny's eyes and saw she wasn't a monster. He saw something else too. He couldn't be sure what it was. But it was the way she was looking at him. That she was okay. That she did care about the club, even cared about him.

'Let's talk when you can.' Penny handed him her card. 'Phone number and email. You choose when. I know things are tough.'

'Do you?'

Penny nodded. 'If there's anything I can do...'

'Thanks. But how do you know? Do you mean about Dad?'

'I know he has only weeks to live, yes.'

Roy swallowed. Hearing it from someone else. That was a body blow. He took a deep breath.

'How do you know?' he gasped.

'It's my job to know about you, Roy. That's all. In a good way. Only in a good way, I promise.'

'Right.' Roy glanced round at his dad.

Now the players were coming onto the pitch. The spell was broken.

Roy held the card up and smiled. 'Thanks.'

Penny nodded. 'See you, Roy Race.'

'WE NEED POINTS today,' Johnny Dexter shouted, clapping his hands as the players warmed up pre-match in the Tayir Stadium.

Four days later. Another fixture for Melchester Rovers Men.

'Every game we need points. We need to see the season as a nine-month building of points, to push us up or keep us up the table. Create a gap with the bottom three. You got me?'

Roy and his teammates nodded. They got Johnny Dexter.

Today Melchester Rovers were home to

Dudley Wanderers, only recently relegated from the Premier League. A team of internationals, of superstars from every continent in the world. But a team who had failed collectively the season before. Catastrophically.

'We finish off in this stadium with a bang, okay?' Johnny went on.

'Finish off?' Asif Mirza asked. 'Is this...'

Johnny Dexter raised his hands. 'Er... forget I said that. But remember, this is the last chance we get to show Tynecaster what we are. Until we get at them in the Premier League that is.'

But now most of the players were speculating. They were going back to Mel Park. They'd be home soon. Leaving this vast chasm of steel and floodlights, advertising hoardings and plastic seats without a real footballing soul. How good would that feel?

Mel Park – version two – rebuilt after a fire.
A new era.

Home had been tricky that morning. Dad had had trouble in the night, then in the morning, and Roy had been up and down with him. He had been offered a hotel by the club, so that he could sleep uninterrupted, but he'd said no, that he wanted to be with his dad at home before he headed off to the match.

It had been worth spending the night at home, even though he was shattered. Because, as Roy left for the game, Dad had been sitting up, looking better. A bit better. It was true that he'd not eaten or drunk anything. But he'd not been sick, either. His dose of painkillers had been increased.

Dad was sitting up. There was a TV at the end of the bed. He had the remote by his good hand.

'Will you watch me?' Roy asked. 'It's on the TV.'

He'd not been expecting an answer. None of them did. But it didn't stop him or his sister or his mum from holding one-sided conversations with Dad. Then Dad surprised him. With three words, not one.

'Always, Roy. Always.'

That was Roy's team talk. He didn't need a word from Mouse or Johnny.

He jogged down the ground like he always did, determined to come home with a win, to see a smile on his dad's exhausted face.

The Tayir Stadium. For the last time.

And here they were playing Dudley – who two seasons ago were a so-called top four side and had made it to the final of the Champions League. There were still World Cup Winners in the team, including the French World Footballer of the Year goalkeeper Benjamin Sarraute, who was seeing out his contract so he could leave on a free transfer to a team in China.

Dudley came at Melchester from the off. Forcing the pace. Hammering Rovers' defence.

It was unusual. The way that Melchester Rovers played – fast-paced passing and movement, risk – was often negated by teams that played deep and offered only an occasional attack on the break. But, when Melchester played teams who came at them, it was different. All they needed to do was soak up the pressure, then hit the opposition hard and fast once they'd won back possession.

The plan worked well after just five minutes. With happy results.

Vic Guthrie played a square ball to Jimmy Slade, who, relishing the limelight, skinned two defenders, then nudged the ball wide to Roy as he burst into the area. Roy took the Dudley defence by surprise by playing a swift one-two with Asif Mirza. Then one on one with the world's best goalkeeper, with the defence scattered as if by a strike in ten pin bowling, Roy hammered it home with his right foot.

1–0.

Roy loved open games. The freedom to play football at full pace. It was like being a kid again.

But forty seconds after the restart it was level. Dudley's driving midfielder sliced through Melchester's defence like a knife through butter, then smashed the ball home.

1–1.

Six minutes after that, Mel Rovers were cut open again, with half their defenders destroyed and out of the game by the pace of Dudley's English striker.

1–2.

Roy did his best to rally the team.

'Come on,' he said, gathering his teammates. 'We keep playing like we play. Open football. We'll score more. We just have to try to track back quicker.'

'Track back quicker,' Jimmy Slade raged,

bouncing the ball hard on the ground in a fit of anger. 'We need to keep our shape. It's no wonder other teams' strikers love playing us: they're guaranteed a goal-scoring bonus. Come on.'

'Agreed,' Roy said, wondering if he liked Jimmy's passion for the game, or if it was annoying. 'Let's try and keep it tighter,' he added. He would think about that later.

Then a few minutes of calm. It reminded Roy of two animals that launch into a playfight that becomes too wild, too dangerous and they withdraw a little to judge each other from a distance.

The game was less frenetic now. Half an hour in Rovers earned a corner. They put six players on the edge of the box. Roy saw Dudley's Austrian central defender, Peter Handke, laugh in surprise. Then he prepared for the corner.

Roy had an idea it would be a good corner. At the tail end of the last training session, Roy had watched Jimmy Slade practising taking corners. Even after Roy had changed and was ready to walk home, Slade was still there with a couple of the juniors and one of the groundsmen, still practising his delivery.

Jimmy's corner was – of course – perfection. It soared into the area, then fell into the path of Roy and Will and Lofty Peak, the three of them attacking in a row on the six-yard line.

Roy leaped the highest of the three, reaching the ball, and slammed his forehead down on the ball, which hit the ground two metres in front of the goal line and ricocheted into the roof of the net.

The Tayir Stadium exploded with noise. And – as Roy picked the ball out of the net – Sarraute, the French keeper, clapped him on the back.

'We have never heard noise like this from the Tynecaster fans. They are *magnifique*, your fans, no?'

'Thank you,' Roy gasped.

2–2.

Roy had never felt so in the game before. He was not thinking about home, about his dad, about anything. Just the ball, the team, the points. He needed this. He needed something to go well, unfettered joy.

And things were about to get even better.

Rovers were attacking again. Then Dudley came back at them. End to end until a mistake at the back from Dudley, their defence doing what it had done all season the year before, leading to their unexpected relegation. Patrick Nolan was suddenly one on one with Sarraute. The fans were on their feet. A deep intake of breath. Knees bent in anticipation of the leap into the air to celebrate a goal.

Nolan hammered the ball wide of the keeper, who somehow, miraculously, extended his leg, and blocked the ball to send it hammering hard and fast directly at Roy.

Roy didn't think about it.

It just happened.

He felt himself change the shape of his body, arms out, balanced, right leg forward, knee bent over the ball, then he hit it hard on the volley with his left boot.

Roy span like a top and fell to the turf.

Then he heard the noise. The roar of the crowd. Then around him the voices of his teammates, shouting. Then the speakers. Then the blood pumping in his brain.

And Roy felt complete, this was who he was. Roy of the Rovers. Scorer of a perfect hat-trick against the best goalkeeper in the world.

Roy staggered to his feet and roared with

emotion, punching both his arms into the air, then turning to embrace Patick Nolan to thank him for his part in the goal. Eyes closed, Roy willed the TV camera to pan in onto him so that his dad could see him.

Then a hand on his shoulder, mid-celebration.

Vic's.

'They're subbing you,' Vic shouted through the noise.

'What?'

'You're coming off. Are you hurt?'

Roy shook his head and looked at the pitch side. At Johnny and Mouse. Heard the colossal roar of disapproval from the crowd. Why would they take off such a player? In his moment of glory.

Then silence fell on the Tayir Stadium. The sound of fans saying 'Shhh.' And Roy looked again at Vic Guthrie's face. What was going on? Roy had no idea. The fans. The bench. Vic. Everything was weird. It felt like a dream when things just don't add up.

'Go,' Vic said. 'Maybe…'

Roy didn't hear the rest of what Vic said. He just jogged off the pitch, taking the handshake of one of the Dudley players as he passed him. This, he knew, was no dream: it was a nightmare. A nightmare about to play out.

He jogged in silence. In utter unthinkable silence.

The stadium could have been empty.

But it was worse. The silence of forty thousand fans as Roy heard his feet on the turf, head down.

They knew.

Something at home. Something bad. Something I need to be at home for. I need to get back. To Dad.

Johnny Dexter put his hands on Roy's shoulders and made him look into his eyes. He confirmed Roy's worst fears.

'Roy. Look at me. Listen to me. You need to go home. There's a lift waiting for you outside reception.'

PENNY WAS WAITING in her car outside the Tayir reception when Roy jogged out of the stadium in his full Melchester Rovers kit, boots included.

The world he emerged into was a shock to him. After the noise and lights and colour of the stadium, Melchester city had the look of a post-apocalyptic disaster area. Litter tumbling down empty roads. No cars or trucks anywhere near the fan zone. Just one or two police officers standing like statues. A bleak eerie silence broken only by the sound of a dog barking.

For a moment, Roy stood, confused as to what he should do, where he should go.

'Roy. Let me give you a lift,' Penny called from her car. A Mini.

Roy had been ready to run home, across town. But a lift would get him home quicker. He knew that.

'You'll miss the game,' Roy said, knowing he sounded stupid.

'The game doesn't matter,' Penny muttered.

Roy climbed in, placing his feet carefully so he didn't muddy the floor of the Mini.

Inside it was air conditioned to 20 degrees, a soft breeze on his legs from the vents. Quickly, Roy could smell his own sweat.

He checked a text from his sister

Get home. Now. Dad's not good.

'I'm sorry,' Roy said, embarrassed about his sweatiness. 'I smell.'

Penny shrugged. 'That doesn't matter, either. What matters is getting you home.'

Penny hit the accelerator, a barrier ahead of them lifted and they were into traffic, a horn honking in protest as they cut up a white van. They drove in silence as Roy stared ahead. The adrenaline of the game had disappeared and he felt shattered. He let himself rest for the journey. He closed his eyes.

It took seven minutes of ring road, main road and traffic lights to reach the steep terraced street where Roy had lived all his life with his mum and dad and sister. Penny cut the engine.

'Thanks,' Roy said.

'Go,' Penny said. 'Call me if you need anything. Anything, I said.'

'Thanks,' Roy said. 'I appreciate this.'

Then he climbed out of the car and took a deep breath.

Through the front door.

Up the stairs. Mud coming off his boots, leaving shapes on the carpet. The Macmillan nurse he'd come to know over the last few days – Mike – was at the top of the staircase with a doctor Roy had not seen before.

'Hi,' Roy said to both of them. 'Thanks for being here.'

'He's very close,' Mike replied. 'Go in.'

Roy thanked Mike and looked down the stairs at a trail of mud he had left, then he pushed his parents' bedroom door.

The first thing he saw was the glare of the TV, still showing the game. Then Mum and Rocky – one on either side of the bed – and the image of himself in his Melchester Rovers strip in the mirror in the wardrobe on the far side of the room.

The window was slightly open, bright daylight and fresh air pouring in. The light was off.

His eyes adjusting, Roy saw his dad lying on the bed, head back, mouth slightly open.

Mum stood up, still holding Dad's hand. 'Come and sit here,' she beckoned.

Roy shook his head and squatted beside Rocky.

'I'm fine,' he said. He looked at Rocky.

She smiled, looked deep into his eyes, then, her face crumpling, threw her arms round him. Through her sobs Roy could hear his sister explain. 'He came over all funny soon after you'd gone. We thought he was tired. That's all. Then Mum called Mike as soon as she could. And Mike said...'

'Then the doctor came,' Mum took over. 'And they think this is it,' Mum said. 'This is it, Roy. Now. You understand?'

Roy nodded. He heard the soft voices of the nurse and the doctor in the corridor. Adjusting his position, Roy leaned forward and kissed his dad on the forehead. His eyes were closed. His cheeks looked hollow. His skin was pink. Roy followed his short slow breaths.

'I love you, Dad,' Roy said.

Then the three of them sat there with Dad as the light in the window faded from bright to pale to night, the street lights on. When the doctor reappeared – maybe hours later, maybe minutes, Roy didn't know – she adjusted Dad's bedding, checking his pulse, listening to his breathing.

'He's very calm,' she told them. 'But it's close now.'

Rocky let out a sob, then began to cry. Roy put his arm round her. And she let him. He felt pain in his jaw and realised he had his teeth locked tight.

Mum held one of Dad's hands. Rocky and Roy the other.

They watched Dad's chest rising and falling, heard his breath wheezing. Roy noticed his face changing colour.

'We love you, Danny,' Mum said.

Rocky sobbed.

Roy tightened his jaw more. The pain was a relief. He liked it. It helped him.

'That's it,' Mike said softly after a few moments. 'He's at rest now.'

Mum nodded and breathed out. She held her hands out to Rocky and Roy. Now they gripped each other's hands.

There was nothing to say.

SOME DAYS LATER, Melchester Rovers travelled to London to play Kenilworth Park Rangers. A tough fixture south of the river, where the players were hard and their fans even harder. There had been a break of ten days in the Championship fixtures to make space for another round of international fixtures.

But now the football was back.

The fans were glad of it. And so was Roy Race. Once he was over the line he was a footballer. Not a son or a brother or an ex-boyfriend.

He was a footballer: full stop.

It was a tough game. Roy was thrilled about that. He wanted tough.

End to end under low stands and – in the distance – the tall silver and black monolithic buildings of the City of London. And under the endless flow of aeroplanes dropping out from the clouds like a string of fairy lights.

London. The capital city. He remembered a trip with Dad to London. Rocky with them. They visited HMS *Belfast* on the Thames. It had been amazing.

But Roy knew he had to concentrate on the rectangle of green, lit by floodlights, even though it was only mid-afternoon. Not tall buildings. Not aeroplanes. Not warships.

Suddenly, an explosion of noise came from the home fans, snapping Roy out of his dreaming.

Roy had not played here before, but he had heard that the crowd was like an extra man on the opposition's team. And it felt like it. It was the first time this season he'd been unable to hear the Melchester fans making noise at the far end of the pitch.

And he was glad of them. They brought him back. What had he been doing? He was never normally distracted like this.

Roy was up front, as usual, alongside Will, playing four-four-two. Early in the game, a long ball came from Vic at the centre of midfield. Roy chested it down, turned his back on a defender – a skilful young centre back called Hunter Still – shielded the ball, then played in Will. But his pass was a touch too short and Will had to fly in to try to win the ball.

Will took his defender's trailing leg and found himself with his opponent defender on their hands and knees.

Foul.

A bad tackle from Will. But Roy saw it as a good tackle. Any tackle from Will was progress.

Free kick to Kenilworth.

Roy smiled and clapped Will on the back.

'Good tackle, mate. Get a yellow card and I'll buy you a bag of Haribos on the way home.'

Will laughed. And Roy could tell he was pleased to have his tackling boots back on.

Just before half time – after another surging run from Asif Mirza – the ball span free to Will who nodded it to Roy. Roy took the ball to shield it again, but failed to control it and lost it to that same defender who had been hassling Roy and Will all game. The defender surprised everyone by taking the ball wide with a fast solo run. Failing to catch him, Roy could only watch as the solo run became a three on two, a pinpoint pass and a goal.

1–0.

Roy shook his head.

He had done that. He'd lost the ball, all his teammates in offensive positions. His fault.

He shook his head.

It was still 1–0 to the home team at half time. Roy jogged into the tunnel with his teammates. But, however hard he tried to be angry at himself for causing Rovers to concede, Roy couldn't. There was nothing there. No emotion. No drive.

The second half began in the same way: Kenilworth forcing Melchester back, not letting them play. The only Rovers player having any impact was Jimmy Slade, whose name was being chanted by the Rovers fans.

But to no avail. It was 2–0 after fifty minutes. A Vernon Elliott foul early in the half. A penalty. A goal.

And now Kenilworth were playing deeper, protecting their two-goal lead. Hunter Still, the classy defender, had the whole Melchester attack in his pocket.

With the middle of the park so congested with stubborn defenders and desperate attackers, the next event was inevitable. Another chaos of short passes to try to cut through the defence and the ball span to Roy. Back to goal again, Roy slid the ball to Will. He failed to see Will control it, turn and then have it knocked away from him.

Roy watched what happened next from the floor. As Will's tackler moved away with the ball, Will went in for it again, thumping the ball, causing the Kenilworth player to stumble and crash to the ground.

The referee's whistle blew.

Will stood up as a yellow card was thrust into the air.

Roy and Will's eyes met across the pitch. They shared a secret smile. Will was back. His tackle-shy days were over. And Roy owed his best mate a bag of Haribos. But, still, Roy couldn't feel anything. He knew it was wrong that he wasn't bothered that they were losing 2–0. He started to wonder if he should ask to come off, give his place in the team to someone else.

It was Jimmy Slade who created Melchester Rovers' most memorable moment of the match. Frustrated by the congestion in the centre of the pitch – with no room to make passes – he cut through the Kenilworth midfield and defence, a Maradona-like mazy run that ended with a short pass to Will. A magnificent piece of skill.

Will took the ball, trapped it, then back-heeled it to Roy just as he came into the penalty area. One touch wide with his left foot to evade the last defender, then Roy rebalanced and slid the ball into the net with his right.

Goal.

He'd scored.

Rovers were only 2–1 down now, the away end leaping about, red and yellow scarves and shirts. Roy remembered Dad.

He gave himself a moment to stare up at the sky, the rain hitting his face. He raised his hand and the last conversation he had had with his dad echoed in his mind.

Will you watch me?

Always, Roy. Always.

Roy jogged to the centre circle, following Jimmy Slade who had grabbed the ball and was racing to force a quick restart.

But, after ten more minutes of deep defending from Kenilworth, the referee ended it.

Kenilworth 2 Melchester Rovers 1.

Another defeat.

Sitting on the coach on the way north, Roy didn't think about the defeat or football or even the fact that Will had got his tackling boots back. He was thinking about Monday. At the church. His dad's funeral.

He closed his eyes.

How does that work? Just what were you supposed to do or be like at your dad's funeral?

As he watched four men and women dressed in black suits slide the brown wooden box out of the black hearse and ease it onto their shoulders, Roy was playing a song over and over in his head. It was one of his dad's favourite songs.

Something by Radiohead. He couldn't remember the title, but he only needed a few words.

Fade out… fade out again…

Dad was in the box. Wearing a pair of

jeans and his 1980s Melchester Rovers top. The funeral directors had asked them to choose what he would be wearing for his funeral.

Fade out… fade out again…

The Radiohead song was helping. Repeating that line over and over was keeping other thoughts and emotions out of Roy's head. If he sang it loud enough on the inside.

The churchyard was cold. Cloud cover and early autumn winds made it feel like winter. The trees were already shedding heavy wet leaves. A shower of rain had darkened the tree trunks and gravestones that the mourners were standing around. It was a bleak setting.

There were red and yellow flowers on the brown box. And Dad's Rovers scarf.

An unwelcome thought about the scarf and whether it should be in the coffin or not came into Roy's head. Maybe Dad should have it with him? It might get lost. It might fall off.

Stupid thoughts.

Fade out... fade out again...

It was too late to change where the scarf went. He had to let that go now.

Roy glanced at the crowds of people standing by the entrance to the church. More black. Black suits. Black dresses. Black hats and jackets and cardigans. Then the odd flash of red and yellow. Rovers scarves.

Roy smiled at the people. Well, he hoped it looked like a smile.

He saw Mouse and Hamish and Penny and Johnny and Lofty and Will and Vernon and Vic and Duncan and Gordon and family friends. Fred and Rover. There were hundreds of people here. All to pay their respects to Dad. Too much. This was too much. Roy bit into his lip until he could taste blood. Until he could taste something, anyway.

Fade out... fade out again...

Then he saw Paco. Paco Diaz. He must have travelled all the way from Spain. Just to pay his respects to Roy's dad. Roy gasped and started to raise his hand to wave at Paco, who nodded, solemn, sombre to him. But Roy realised his hand was being held.

Mum. He was holding Mum's hand.

So Roy raised his other hand and put his thumb up to his Spanish friend. He was so shocked. What a gesture from Paco! It was too much. Why were people so kind? Why couldn't they stop being so kind?

Now Roy saw Paco gesture to his side with his eyes. A subtle move he'd seen him do on the football pitch. At Rocky.

How could he forget about his family? This was the strangest day. A private family drama of the most intense kind all played out as your friends and people you know stand there watching you, all dressed in black.

Roy felt a flash of anger. Towards the mourners. And he knew it was wrong. But he didn't let it go. He kept the anger inside him. It stopped him breaking down.

The Radiohead line. His anger. Making his teeth crack. He'd do anything to keep his head together.

Roy could see what Paco had seen. That Rocky's eyes looked wild. Like when she lost it on the pitch and was about to get a red card. She was motionless. But her eyes looked insane.

Leaving Mum to speak to her brother, Roy's uncle Rob, Roy edged across the stage – or what felt like a stage – to Rocky.

He put his hand on her shoulder and she turned to him with a look of complete incomprehension on her face.

'What?' she said under her breath. She meant *Get off me. Don't touch me.* But Roy ignored that. It was the look in her eyes. Like she was hypnotised. She had been stood like that – alone – for minutes.

He put a hand on each of her shoulders. She shook her head, warning him off. But he ignored her and took her in both his arms. There was no resistance. In fact, he felt his sister's arms cling to him like she would when they used to go swimming with each other before she could swim properly, when she was two and he was four and her hands would go into his flesh and he would let it happen and not let on that it hurt. Like they were now.

Rocky was juddering now, quaking as she sobbed and sobbed, her head buried in his chest. And Roy held her hard and stared out – not crying, not anything – staring at the city, the moor behind, the terraced houses running up the hill and – there – in the foreground, the new floodlights of Mel Park.

Then Mum's hand on his shoulder.

They stood as a triangle – no longer a square, three not four – and looked at each other in the eye.

'Come on,' Mum said. 'Let's do this for your dad.'

The coffin was going in. They had to follow it. Then everybody else would follow them. Then the service. And the handshakes. And the drinks and food. And then it would be over. Hours from now. Hours and hours.

Fade out… fade out again…

The Race family walked slowly into church. Mum in the middle, holding each of her children's hands. They walked slowly past hard wooden pews and bare stone pillars. There was no light coming through the stained glass windows and the church lights barely troubled the darkness.

Roy didn't catch anyone's eyes. He just stared at his dad's coffin. Is that what you were supposed to do? What was the rule? Did you look at people and smile as you followed your dad's body in a box into a church? Or did you ignore everyone? Was that the right thing? What would he say? Hello... How are you? How's your family?

Fade out... fade out again...

The coffin was already at the front of the church. On a stand. The flowers and his scarf were there. More flowers, spelling out 'DAD'.

Roy swore to himself.

They walked to the coffin and Roy felt his mum's weight shift, so he put his arm around her. He could feel Rocky's arm around her too. They were holding her up. That was the truth. Without them she'd be on the floor.

Together, brother and sister eased their mum back to the pews or benches or whatever they call the things you sit on when you're at your dad's funeral.

Then they sat down. Roy glanced at his mum and sister. They were staring dead ahead.

Roy swallowed and stared ahead too. His heart felt like it was beating so fast it would explode. He felt sick. He checked his mum. She had not fainted. She turned to him and half smiled. He tried to half smile back. And Roy realised she was a widow. His mum was a widow.

27

THE SERVICE BEGAN with a song. A well-known hymn that Roy had heard in churches a hundred times. He was surprised he knew it word for word.

The two or three hundred mourners, all behind Roy and his mum and sister, sang along, the voices of those who were just singing quietly occasionally broken by the sound of someone who was used to singing in church. The kind of thing Roy and Rocky normally would have laughed about. Normally.

Then at the end of the hymn, the vicar

looked at the front pews, at Roy and Rocky and Mum. And then she nodded at Mum.

Mum stood up.

'What are you doing, Mum?' Roy whispered.

'Kathleen Race will now say a few words about her husband, Danny,' the vicar answered Roy's question as Mum made her way to the front, looking back at her children with a faint smile.

Roy was stunned. He watched as his mum walked the few steps to the front. He noticed she had no notes. And tried to remember if he had ever seen her speak in public. He hadn't. Not once. That was because she hated public speaking. If anything like this had come up before, Dad had done the public speaking.

So why was she doing this?

Roy and Rocky caught each other's eyes as Mum stumbled, grabbed onto the stone font at the front of the church, steadied herself and tried to smile at the crowd now facing her.

Then as Mum stared into the crowd for a few seconds, Roy half sat, half stood, worrying that he had to go to her aid. Noticing that Rocky was in exactly the same position.

Until Mum began to speak.

'Out and about, my husband – Roy and Rocky's father, the man you knew as Danny Race – was always the same. A good man. A kind man. He'd do anything for anyone. You all know that.'

There was a murmur of agreement from behind Roy as he watched his mum grow in confidence. She took a deep breath.

'Inside our home,' she went on, 'he was the same. You all knew him in whichever way you knew him. I don't need to tell you stories about him. You have your own stories and memories. I hope those memories and stories keep you going today and as time moves on in a world without Danny Race.'

Mum paused. Roy tried to ignore the weight of the words his mum was saying.

A world without Danny Race. A world without Dad.

'I am lucky that I have the two children

Danny and I brought up to remind me of what a decent man he was. He might not be here anymore – but they are.'

Mum gazed lovingly at Rocky and Roy. Roy looked back at her and tried to gaze lovingly back. But he was so busy keeping his face rigid to avoid breaking down, his face must have looked pretty strange.

Another deep breath.

'Roy and Rocky are footballers. They are young adults. They are friends to their friends. They are brother and sister. But they are more than that. So much more.

'Over the three years since Danny was first diagnosed with his terrible disease to his last day last week, both my children have been my rocks. Since their mid-teens, they have done more than I would have dreamed young people would do. They were there for their dad. They are here for me. Young people that age should not have to do what they did and should not have to see a parent go through what their dad went through. But they did. And – rather than be a worry to me and their dad, making things harder – they made things easier. They helped in every way they could, but continued to live their own lives. Lives that their father was so proud of and excited by. That – if anything – during these times, gave him happiness. To see his children flourish. He was prouder than proud of them. For that I thank them.'

Roy looked down at his hands. He twisted his fingers and drove his heel into the stone floor of the church.

Mum glanced up at her audience and smiled.

'I'll stop soon. But I want to say one more thing.'

She hesitated.

'We spent a lot of time over the last sixteen years as a family, together. In the car on journeys to see family, or on holiday. Sat in a row at Mel Park with our season tickets. Watching TV shows together in the front room. But – for me – when I think of us as a family, I think of our kitchen table. The four of us, sat facing each other. Arguing. Laughing. Teasing.'

Mum stopped speaking. Took another breath. Put up her hand.

Rocky stood up, then sat down.

'I'm okay. I can do this,' Mum said. 'The kitchen table became the place where we were as family as a family can be and I will always cherish what we had. What do they say? Better to have loved and lost than never to have loved at all?'

Mum coughed, then glanced at the vicar. 'That's it,' she whispered.

The vicar smiled and Mum began to walk back to join the front of the congregation.

That was when Roy realised Rocky was clapping. And that dozens of others had joined in and were standing. Roy stood too as Mum joined them and Roy took her arm as she slumped down in her seat, between him and Rocky.

28

ROY COULDN'T REMEMBER the last time he was alone in the house. But today he was. And it was the strangest feeling.

Empty rooms.

No listening for his dad or his mum needing his help.

No sound from a TV or a radio.

No Mum reading to Dad.

No banging and crashing from Rocky's room.

No food or drink smells from the kitchen.

Nothing, except the central heating cooling down – *click click click* – after it had been on for the morning.

That was finished.

Rocky and Mum had gone to Oxford to stay with Uncle Rob and his little girl, Molly, who they'd not seen for ages. They'd gone with him after the funeral. Penny had said that Roy could take some time off and join them. Compassionate leave, she called it. But Roy said he wanted to get back to work.

To football.

He was finding that football was the only thing keeping him sane. When everything around him was so strange and unsettling, football kept him steady. Football on the radio. Match of the Day. Even playing FIFA. And, of course, real football. That's why he wanted to get out of the empty house and down to Mel Park.

Roy backed out of the front door, rucksack over his shoulder, headphones on, pulled the door to and pushed it to check it had locked. Then he turned around to face the day to see four figures at the end of the path.

Lofty Peak.

Vic Guthrie.

Will Gray.

Paco Diaz.

All in Melchester Rovers tracksuits. Expect for Paco, who was in casual trousers, a jumper and a jacket.

'What are you lot doing here?' Roy asked, looking to see where they'd parked their cars. Mum's car space – the disabled bay still painted onto the tarmac – was empty.

And his mind drifted – like it always seemed to drift – and he wondered when the council would come to remove the parking bay. Did they do it immediately or leave the family time to grieve? What a stupid question! His mind was so full of thoughts like that. He hated it. That's why he needed football.

'Come to walk in with you,' Lofty said.

Roy knew what this was. It was kindness. It was friendship. But he also knew he didn't want it. He wanted normal. He wanted football.

He pulled his headphones off and put them round his neck, nodded at his mates and began to walk down the hill towards the canal and Mel Park.

'You didn't have to do that,' he muttered, trying to be polite.

'Everyone else would've been here,' Vic said. 'But we eventually agreed to limit it to four.'

Will, Lofty and Paco laughed uneasily.

'Really, I'm fine...'

Roy felt Lofty's huge hand on his shoulder. He stopped and looked at his friend who was staring into his eyes, mournfully, meaningfully.

'We're your mates,' Will added. 'You don't have to pretend to be fine around us, got it?'

Roy tried to smile. He wanted to get off the subject. Of Dad. Of death. Of grief.

Roy glanced at Vic. He had said nothing so far and wasn't looking Roy in the eye like the other three were. Then there he was, eye to eye, uncomfortable. Very Vic Guthrie.

'You were there for me,' Vic said.

Roy stopped again and looked at his four friends. What could he say to warn them off? But without hurting their feelings?

This was tricky. Everything was tricky.

'Thanks, Vic,' Roy said. 'Thanks, Lofty, lads. I appreciate it. But really… you don't have to worry about me. I'm okay.'

Roy saw Will and Lofty glance at each

other. He could see they weren't buying it.

'I just want to get on with things, you know. Get back to normal. To football.'

Roy saw his friends nod, take his feelings on board. But were they really hearing him?

'Just football,' Roy insisted. 'Do you understand? That's what I need now.'

His friends nodded and they began to walk down the hill to Mel Park. Four doors down, the postwoman appeared. Roy knew her well. How many times had he opened the door to her and taken a parcel or seen her on his street as he was out for a run? She stopped Roy, placing her hand gently on his shoulder. Roy's teammates walked on and waited a few steps away.

'I just wanted to tell you, Roy, how sorry I am. About your dad. Please pass on my love to your mum? And your sister, yeah?'

'I will,' Roy tried to smile. 'Thank you.'

'It's a tough time. Let me know if I can help. Anything. Just ask.'

'I will, thanks.'

The postwoman went on her way and Roy jogged to catch up with his teammates, seeing one of his neighbours waving to him across the road.

Roy waved back.

'Nice neighbourhood,' Paco commented as they began to walk down the hill again. 'Nice people.'

'Yeah,' Roy said. 'We're lucky. We've got our street. We've got Melchester.'

'That can help you, no?' Paco asked.

'Yeah,' and Roy smiled a real smile. 'It does. And so do you lot. You're my teammates. And you're here for me. That means a lot. Thanks, lads.'

Thank you

Huge thanks to Bobby and Olivia at Rebellion for their support with *Sudden Death*. And to Rob Williams for the powerful first scenes in *New Digs* that I adapted to be hopefully powerful final scenes in this book. Thank you as well to Tamsin Shelton for her copy-editing and proofreading help.

Thanks to Simon Robinson, as always, for his advice throughout.

This book is dedicated to my dad, Peter Nokes, who suffered what Roy's dad suffers in this book. I was a similar age to Roy when these events happened in my family. It was tough. But I have kind of enjoyed bringing those memories back to write *Sudden Death*. I think – when it is the right time – that it can be a good thing to write about things that have been painful in the past or present. It doesn't have to be a novel. It can be a diary or a poem. It can be public or private. Whatever works for you. So here's to Peter Nokes. He liked books. Now he's in one.

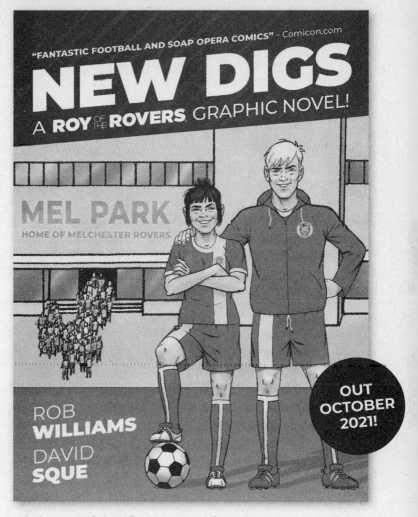

ILLUSTRATED FICTION
SEASON 1

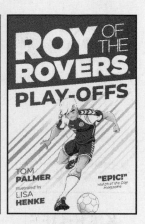

SCOUTED

Author: Tom Palmer
Illustrator: Lisa Henke

ISBN: 978-1-78108-698-8

Roy Race is the most talented striker in Melchester – but is he good enough to catch the eye of the Melchester Rovers scouts?

TEAMWORK

Author: Tom Palmer
Illustrator: Lisa Henke

ISBN: 978-1-78108-707-7

Life gets tricky for Roy as he adjusts to life in the spotlight. Fortune and glory await, but can Roy juggle football, fame and family?

PLAY-OFFS

Author: Tom Palmer
Illustrator: Lisa Henke

ISBN: 978-1-78108-722-0

Crunch time for Rovers: the end of the season is here, the club is in deep trouble, and it's down to Roy to bring a bit of hope back to the Melchester faithful.

READ? ☐   **READ?** ☐   **READ?** ☐

GRAPHIC NOVELS
S E A S O N 1

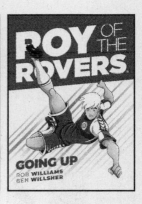

KICK-OFF

Writer: Rob Williams
Artist: Ben Willsher

ISBN: 978-1-78108-652-0

Roy Race is 16, talented, and desperate to make it as a footballer. But is he good enough for Melchester Rovers? Now's the time to prove if he's got what it takes to become Roy of the Rovers.

FOUL PLAY

Writer: Rob Williams
Artist: Ben Willsher

ISBN: 978-1-78108-669-8

Roy picks up an injury that puts him on the sidelines, and suddenly there's competition for his place as a brand new - and brilliant - striker is brought in by the management...

GOING UP

Writer: Rob Williams
Artist: Ben Willsher

ISBN: 978-1-78108-673-5

Roy and the team have battled through a tough season, but have they got enough left to get promoted? Or will they fall at the final hurdle and see the club sold by its greedy owner?

READ? ☐   **READ?** ☐   **READ?** ☐

ILLUSTRATED FICTION
SEASON 2

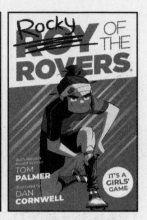

ON TOUR

Author: Tom Palmer
Illustrator: Dan Cornwell

ISBN: 978-1-78108-685-8

Roy Race is living the dream. But something strange is afoot, and as Rovers head off on a preseason tour, Roy is treated differently, and kept apart from the team. What's going on?

READ? ☐

FROM THE ASHES

Author: Tom Palmer
Illustrator: Dan Cornwell

ISBN: 978-1-78108-783-1

Mel Park lies in ruins. Dodgy backroom deals brought Rovers low, and now Roy is determined to lift it out of the mess it's in. But he might have to break a few rules to do it...

READ? ☐

ROCKY

Author: Tom Palmer
Illustrator: Dan Cornwell

ISBN: 978-1-78108-826-5

Rocky's sick of everyone knowing her through Roy. It's time to find her own way as a person and a player and she's going to need all her grit and determination to do it...

READ? ☐

GRAPHIC NOVELS
SEASON 2

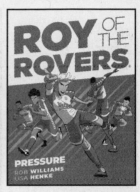

TRANSFERRED

Writer: Rob Williams
Artist: Lisa Henke

ISBN: 978-1-78108-750-3

Roy tries to adjust to his
new life, while Melchester
defy the odds and top
the table, but behind
the scenes chaos ensues
thanks to Melchester's
unscrupulous chairman
Barry 'Meat' Cleaver...

ALL TO PLAY FOR

Writer: Rob Williams
Artist: Lisa Henke

ISBN: 978-1-78108-756-5

Melchester Rovers have
sunk to the bottom of
the table and things are
looking desperate! For
any other team relegation
would seem like an
absolute certainty...

PRESSURE

Writer: Rob Williams
Artist: Lisa Henke

ISBN: 978-1-78108-764-0

Having had their thirty
point deduction rescinded,
Melchester Rovers find
themselves back in the
top half of the table with
a chance of promotion to
the Championship.

READ? ☐

READ? ☐

READ? ☐

SUPPORT YOUR CHILD'S READING SKILLS
THROUGH FOOTBALL

FOR PARENTS

Here are some top tips to get your kids excited about reading and writing using the power of football!

Become a football detective

Challenge your child to find out as much as they can about their favourite footballer: their age, their best goal celebration – even their most famous haircut! Encourage them to find out fun facts about their favourite player by searching for information online, reading football magazines and visiting the library.

It's ok to substitute a book that isn't match fit

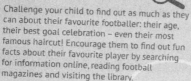

Don't force your child to finish a book they aren't enjoying. Go to your local library and let your child try out lots of different styles and ways of reading – from autobiographies and audiobooks, to novels and ebooks.

Turn reading into a team effort

Reading together with your child, even after they can read for themselves, helps you bond, share stories together and shows your child that stories are important, powerful and – above all – fun!

Write your way into football history

Football is filled with magical moments, difficult decisions, opinions and statistics. After a big game, help your child use their love of football to write a match report, a blog (lots of top ballers have these), a newspaper article or a script for an online video about what happened.

Don't show reading the red card

All types of reading counts, so if your child enjoys reading online, reading comics, graphic novels, magazines, as well as books, that's good too! Ask your child's teacher or your local library for recommendations that will get your child excited about reading.

Support Team Reading!

Donate to the National Literacy Trust to give the gift of reading. Visit **literacytrust.org.uk/donate** to support their work in the UK's most disadvantaged communities, working with families and children to raise literacy levels giving them the skills they need to succeed.

National Literacy Trust

Changing life stories

Visit wordsforlife.org.uk for more family reading and writing activities

Registered charity no. 1116260 (England and Wales) and SC042944 (Scotland)

FINISHED READING THIS COMIC?
WHAT CAN YOU DO NEXT?

FOR KIDS

Discover ways your love of football can help you improve your skills in class

What happens next?

Why not continue the story of this book once you've finished it? Try and write an extra chapter about what you think the characters do next.

Write a review of this book to share with your friends

What did you think of this book? How many stars out of five would you give the plot and why? Put on your thinking cap and write a short review of what you have read so your friends can see what you particularly liked about it.

Share the story with your family

Take to the living room stage and try reading this book out loud to someone at home. It's a great way to practise your reading – and acting! Remember to speak nice and clearly.

Create your own comic strip

What's your favourite part of football? The songs, the teamwork or maybe even the team talks? Pick something you love about football and create your own story in a comic strip.

Write a thank you letter

Show the person who bought you this book how much you appreciate the gift and write them a thank you letter. You can practise your best professional autograph at the end of it too!

Keepy uppy with your reading

Visit your local library to explore all kinds of different sporting magazines and books if you've found this one interesting.

National Literacy Trust

Changing life stories

Visit wordsforlife.org.uk for more family reading and writing activities

YOUR REVIEWS MATTER!

Enjoy this book? Got something to say?
Leave a review on Amazon, GoodReads or with your
favourite bookseller and let the world know!